THE
SYNCOPATED
HEART

A NOVEL

Douglas J. Keeling

outskirts
press™

Outskirts Press, Inc.
http://www.outskirtspress.com

ISBN: 978-1-9772-2852-9

Library of Congress Control Number: 2020912265

Cover Image by Douglas J. Keeling

Outskirts Press and the "OP" logo are trademarks belonging to Outskirts Press, Inc.

PRINTED IN THE UNITED STATES OF AMERICA

For Susie,
ma chérie

Part One

Dying in Paris

ONE

Death came to visit on Tuesday. Pulled into the parking lot in his red Porsche Boxster, top down, and backed into a handicap parking space. He checked his reflection in the rearview mirror, tossed off the seat belt and raised his lanky frame fluidly out of the car. He flicked the door shut with his fingertips and pointed the key fob at the fender, eliciting a double-chirp from beneath the hood. He pocketed the keys, pulled at the lapels of his grey suit and adjusted the knot of his tie. He ran a hand through his silver hair, squinted up in the general direction of the sun, and strode into the building through the glass front doors, which slid away to either side with a barely audible hiss as he approached.

He moved with purpose through the large atrium of the lobby, and took an elevator to the third floor. As he emerged, he paused, as if to mentally prepare himself for his routine. His "rounds" as he referred to them. He then systematically wandered down each corridor, back and forth, on each of the third through tenth floors. He glanced into rooms with their doors standing open, occasionally pausing to rest his hand on the metal handle of a closed door. His pale blue eyes scanned room numbers as he walked, his fingers sometimes lightly touching the dark wood molding that ran waist-high along the corridors. He liked this place, all sleek glass and heavy wood. Very modern and austere. Sterile. More than once he placed the palm of his hand, fingers splayed, on the gray plastic box mounted on the wall next to each room containing the patient records, pausing slightly as if listening for faint sounds in the quiet, carpeted hallway.

On the top floor, near the end of his journey, he entered a room, quietly opening the partially closed door. He stood at the foot of the bed, watching a very elderly woman as she slept. She made quiet noises, small expirations of air between her pale lips, and he observed her in silence. His slender fingers caressed the hard plastic which encased the frame at the foot of the bed, his hand coming to rest on the clean white sheets. The woman stirred, rotating her head slightly, moving her white hair across the surface of the pillow. Then she stilled, slipping back into the depths of sleep. He pulled at the edge of the sheet where it hung along the bed frame, smoothing it down on the edge of the mattress, patted it twice, then turned and left the room, pulling the door back into its semi-closed position behind him.

TWO

The bullet, from a NATO 7.62x39mm round with a 122-grain projectile, left the muzzle of the Kalashnikov AK-104 rifle at a velocity of 1,555 feet per second, spinning from the barrel rifling with a 1-in-9.45-inch twist. It smashed through the wooden back slats of a chair, which altered the shape and trajectory of the copper-jacketed missile slightly. It tore through the fabric of the woman's light jacket and the white silk of her blouse, piercing her skin just below and behind her right breast. It nicked a rib, throwing it into a tumble as it tore through the tissue of her right lung, and into the right ventricle of her heart, crushing the tricuspid valve. It spun forward, expanding as it advanced, exiting the heart through the lower portion of the left ventricle and continuing on through the left lung. It then chipped out a section of the fifth rib and burst out through the left chest wall, leaving behind a gaping exit wound roughly three inches in diameter. It traveled through the air another twenty-four feet, punching a hole through some tinted plate glass and smashing a 12-by-16-inch window pane before lodging in the wood frame of a glass-fronted pastry case. The woman slumped forward onto the small table in front of her, causing it to topple under her weight, falling with her toward the ground. Her chair, with the damaged back slats, slid sideways from beneath her, spinning off to her left and under the adjacent table. She was dead before she hit the sidewalk, before the chair had stopped rotating.

THREE

Life is like a train, it keeps moving. Occasional stops, some scheduled, some not, but mostly moving forward. The trick is to enjoy the ride, not miss too much of the scenery, and not fall or get thrown off the train. That last part can be a bitch. Mostly, you simply keep moving forward. Clickity-clack.

Paris had never been on my destination list. My original plan was to visit the "Bs"; Brussels, Berlin, Barcelona, Bath, Belfast, maybe throw in Amsterdam for a lark. It was supposed to be a very random and spontaneous journey. An odyssey of sorts. The City of Light only became part of the equation when Miranda and her boyfriend Paul offered to let me hitch a ride with them to there from Bonn. It seemed like a good idea at the time. They had a 4-door black-over-red Mini, which by European standards, was practically a motor-home, with plenty of room for me.

They picked me up at an agreed-upon street corner very early in the morning, where I stood rubbing my hands together and pacing back and forth to stay warm in the chilly pre-dawn air. My breath formed a weak cloud of vapor under the pale streetlamp. As it approached, theirs was the only car I had seen on the street during my 20-minute wait.

I greeted them, grabbed my backpack from where it leaned against the lamppost and piled with it into the rear seat of the Mini. I was looking forward to the trip. I had no pending reservations or agendas, and I could pick up on my list of the "Bs" where I had left off at any time. It felt like an impromptu adventure from my long-past youth. The more the merrier, off to La Ville de Lumière.

I'd been rolling around the Continent on my Eurail pass for the better part of three weeks when I accepted their offer and detoured to Paris. I guess you can't really describe it as a detour when I had no set itinerary to begin with.

Paul and Miranda were an interesting pair. I became acquainted with them at a tavern in Bonn, where I was disputing the amount of my bar tab with the proprietor, and Miranda intervened, perhaps saving me from a night in the local hoosegow, or more likely a rude German tongue-lashing. And in retrospect, the tab had probably been accurate.

Miranda was French by nationality, but had been studying the law at the University of Bonn. She was slight but athletically built, looking like she could have been the captain of her school's field hockey team. You could see the fine bone structure of her face emerging from beneath the still-roundish features of youth. A spritely demeanor combined with a serious intelligence and a playful sense of humor made her a joy to interact with.

Paul was American, a recent graduate of Tufts Medical School, and the perfect bookend to the set; the handsome doctor-type in the tradition of Dr. Kildare or George Clooney, depending on your generation. Tall, sandy-haired and blue-eyed, an All-American kid in a California sort of way. He too looked like he had been the captain of a sport, in his case most likely tennis or lacrosse. He was pleasant and comfortable to be around, as long as one was okay with long silences and short, focused conversations. He embodied the philosophy of not speaking unless there was something important to say.

The drive was entertaining. Paul drove most of the way and Miranda and I talked about "the law". It was still a fascinating and philosophical construct to her, and I tried not to let thirty-plus years of reality jade my opinions, or dissuade her enthusiasm.

Driving into Paris is different from entering most other large metropolitan cities by car. You move seamlessly from a rural to urban setting, with increasingly more traffic and buildings which surround you so gradually that you hardly notice the transition.

I watched with interest as we progressed from the outskirts into the older parts of the city. The streets narrowed and the buildings crowded in upon them. By the time we had reached the traditional Parisian neighborhoods, the streets were more like one-way cobblestone alleys, lined on one side by cars parked halfway onto the narrow sidewalks, and on the other by an endless line of scooters and motorcycles parked along the opposite curb. Paul appeared to be unintimidated by the gauntlet, but he didn't attack the narrow lanes with the same abandon as the native drivers.

Miranda directed him to a hostel, pointing out the facade of an unmarked building with black double-doors. She instructed him to pull up in front, which he did, effectively blocking traffic from either direction. I thanked them for the ride, and we hurriedly exchanged cell phone numbers, promising to keep in touch. As I extricated myself from the car to the sound of multiple horns bleating, Miranda made the offer of a home-cooked French meal in her mother's kitchen on Sunday, if I stuck around that long. I said I would let her know. I dragged my backpack out of the rear seat of the Mini and waved them on their way.

The hostel was nice, typical of what I had found so far on the trip. It was a "mom and pop" operation, located in a large, old family home, with the entire upstairs converted into a spacious sleeping dorm and communal bathroom. This particular dorm had ten single beds, lined up side-by-side against the two longer walls. There were three big fans hanging from the high ceilings, and huge multi-paned windows along the street-side wall, making for plenty of air and light in the room. The front of the house on the lower level was comprised of a sitting room full of gaudy, dated furniture, an ancient stone fireplace and a small desk in the corner that served as a reception area.

A large, commercially-equipped kitchen and dining area connected the front of the house to a rear addition, which was where I assumed the hosts lived. It was clean, reasonably well-kept and comfortable, but not fancy, and it had a free Wi-Fi connection. Completely adequate.

I checked myself in with the host husband, hauled my backpack up the narrow wooden stairway, situated my things, and then set about the most important initial task in any major European city: figuring out the subway system. Forty minutes later I had located the nearest Metro station where I could acquire a 5-day Metro pass. A teenage girl in a small booth near the entrance of the station took my photo, in exchange for a few of my Euros, and then the Metro attendant used the photograph of my face to prepare and print my pass. I examined the card before stowing it in my pocket, and couldn't help but think that the grim visage staring back at me from beneath the plastic cover didn't look at all familiar.

FOUR

With most of the day remaining, I set out for a couple of the typical first-time tourist destinations in Paris: the Eiffel Tower and the Arc de Triomphe. The weather was unusually warm for that time of year, so even though it was the off-season, sightseeing was at a premium; tourists of every size, shape, color and nationality crowded the Metro, strolled the narrow streets and lavish boulevards, gawked at the sights and took photos with their phones. I opted out of the Eiffel Tower experience based on the tremendously long line that snaked back and forth below the structure, spilling out onto the sidewalk in front. The Arc de Triomphe would have to satisfy me for the day.

Let me make two initial observations about Paris; number one: Paris is full of beautiful women. And number two: Paris is full of beautiful women. My stroll down the Champs-Élysées included sightings of no fewer than a dozen model-types; six-foot in flats, 108 pounds soaking wet, cheekbones chiseled from granite, smoldering eyes and perfect hair. And no makeup. Au naturel, and absolutely breathtaking. The rest of the other 500 women I perused could hold their own as well. It's hard to pin down the "French" look; hair of varying colors and textures, tall and short, dark and fair, languid and perky. Most of it seemed to be attitude, and knowing how to put their distinctive look together. Thin or full-figured, gorgeous or plain, they all have a certain *"je ne sais quoi"*, to borrow their phrase. Not that I was 100% sure that every woman I ogled was French, there were assuredly representatives from all over Europe, and the world for that matter, strolling the shops and perched in the cafes along the Champs-Élysées. But I felt like I could distinguish the French women by their eyes: weighted with a certain sadness and disdain, yet ready to dance with amusement, or bemusement, at the slightest provocation. Perhaps it's in their DNA, or is a culmination of their historical experience, but those furtive glances can cut you to the core or swallow you up in a fraction of a second.

My further exploration of Paris quickly ate up the rest of my day, and I rumbled back to the hostel on a Metro car crowded with daily commuters. As I rode the escalator up from the bowels of the subway station, I heard an all-too-familiar "ding" erupt from my pocket. An email notification, a sound I had come to dread over the years of being tethered electronically to the rest of the world. Text messages (a different sound) were usually welcome, as I shared my cell phone number with only close friends and family, but the email notification sound had eventually created a Pavlovian sense of dread which permeated much of my professional life. I ignored the sound and the message. I surfaced to the streets among the shuffling crowd and walked for a block along Rue des Abbesses before resting my shopping bags on a window ledge and pulling out my phone to look at the email notification. My former wife. Reminding me about something important, no doubt. I pushed a button to blacken the screen, dropped the phone back into my pocket and pressed on.

My hostel was located in the upper reaches of the Montmartre section of Paris, near the border between the 9th and 18th Arrondissements, one of the highest areas of the city, and the walk was steeply uphill most of the way. I stopped after a couple more blocks to rest, nearly out of breath, and wondered to myself: who was this old man that I'd brought along on the trip, and why did he seem to be following me everywhere? I gave the old guy a talking-to in my head and told him to back off and keep his distance, but I hadn't progressed more than a couple of hundred yards before he caught up with me again. Son of a bitch. Go home. Or just go away. By the time I reached the hostel he'd climbed up onto my back and was riding me like a horse. I collapsed into a chair in the entryway and caught my breath.

Later, after resting for a while, I lounged around the dining room table at the hostel for a good chunk of the evening and had a few beers with the other guests. Afterward, I ascended to the sleeping dorm to settle in for the night. I methodically went through my usual routine, unwinding my phone charger and looking for an electrical outlet, digging out my euro-converter and plugging it in, and stowing my backpack under the bunk. As I connected my phone to the charger the screen lit up and I again saw the email notification icon. I sighed and opened the message on the screen. It was short and direct: "The kids haven't heard from you in almost a week. Let them know you're still alive- Patty."

I felt guilty. It's not like I'd abandoned anyone, my children were all grown, two of them had kids of their own, and the other was living the life of a session musician in New York. But somehow the message made me feel like a bad father. I'm neither Jewish nor Catholic, but I had somehow gotten the "guilt thing" in spades. I leaned the phone against the baseboard, and started emptying my pockets. I froze as my hand swept back to my rear pocket for my wallet, a move so automatic that it caused a flash of panic when it did not go as expected. My hand slapped the empty pocket a second and third time, just making sure, but there was nothing between my hand and ass except denim and cotton. I looked down at the floor next to my phone, but there was nothing there. "Goddammit" was my immediate ineloquent thought. I continued to do a little dance, stepping from side to side, looking at the floor, on the bed, stooping to peer into the space underneath.

"Goddammit," I muttered out loud as I sat down on the

sagging mattress. I mentally reviewed my actions of that afternoon. I'd only made two purchases that I would have had my wallet out for, both at the Monoprix on the Champs-Élysées. I'd been careful about keeping my wallet in my hand or in my pocket, not setting it down on the counter, and I didn't recall varying from that precaution either time. I'd also stopped for a snack and a drink at the Charles V Bistro, but I didn't remember anything out of the ordinary with that transaction either. I laid back on the bed, massaging my eyes, and tried to visualize any part of the afternoon that had been discordant in any way.

Slowly, a moment emerged from the fog of unconscious memory and came into focus. I had been going through a Metro turnstile after swiping my pass, with shopping bags in my hands. In front of me, the train departure alarm sounded, and I thought to myself that I could make the train if I could just get my bags untangled from the arms of the turnstile. I felt some pressure on my back and sensed frustration from the person behind me as the train doors slid shut ten feet in front of us. I half-turned to apologize to the guy following me, but he made an immediate left and slid quickly out the exit gate. I remembered thinking it odd that he was so fast about it; after all, there would be another train in a few minutes. I recalled shrugging and thinking something about the "impatient French". But, as it turned out, the only thing he had been impatient about was bumping my hip pocket, sliding out the wallet and beating it through the exit.

I squinted my eyes at the ceiling and tried to recall the incident visually. I had actually seen the culprit, at least in my peripheral vision. A kid, maybe eighteen or nineteen. Dark, curly hair, non-descript clothing, slight in stature. Dark coloring and eyes. Suddenly the word "gypsy" popped into my head. I recognized that there were all sorts of prejudices and assumptions that went along with that term, but the general impression fit. "Roma" was the European reference, as I recalled. I realized at that moment that I would recognize the kid if I saw him again. Not that such was likely.

I sat up and did a mental inventory of what had been in the wallet; credit cards, my debit card, cash, Automobile Association of America and health insurance cards, and my Oregon driver's license. The good news was that my passport and Eurail pass were tucked away safely in my backpack, along with a small stash of money and one "emergency" credit card, which under the current circumstances had been a great bit of travel planning. A small sense of relief swept over me. At least I had my bare essentials in place.

My next thought was to file a police report, but I dismissed that almost immediately as an exercise in futility. Given all the warnings that I had seen in various Paris locations during my brief time there, pickpocketing was evidently rampant. They probably processed thousands of reports a day, and were unable to do anything about most of them.

I leaned sideways on the bed, and tried to plan in light of my situation. I would need to cancel the cards and get my hands on some more cash, both easily accomplished with my phone and remaining credit card. My travel would not be affected, as my passport and rail pass were still in my possession. I considered the possibility that this might cut my trip short. It didn't have to. I could have new credit cards sent to me, and cash was so accessible electronically that it was almost frightening. I pulled my legs up onto the bed and dropped my head onto the hard pillow. Maybe I'd just sleep on it. Maybe things would look better in the morning light. I drifted off to sleep fully clothed, with the image of the gypsy kid dancing behind my eyes.

FIVE

I am standing at the edge of a precipice. It is a limestone bluff overlooking a small lake created by mining operations from years past, abandoned and filled with water over the subsequent decades. The warm sky is robin's egg blue, scattered with wispy white clouds. A soft wind whistles along the ridge, just cool enough to raise the hairs on the back of my neck.

"It's not that far," says a voice at my shoulder. My older brother Carl. "You just have to make sure you clear the edge, jump far enough out. The water's deep."

I hesitate. I have no idea how far the drop to the water is, but it looks like a mile to my ten-year-old eyes. Carl moves his shoulder forward, nudging it against my bare back.

"Pussy," he says quietly, taunting me.

I calculate the jump in my mind, envisioning the outward thrust necessary to propel me past the lip of limestone that juts out from the base of the cliff below, at the water's edge. I am not afraid, at least not in the understanding of that emotion I have at the age of ten. I am worried; about the distance, about how cold the water might be, about what Carl will think if I refuse to jump. His approval is as necessary as oxygen to me. But I am not afraid.

I close my eyes, gathering my courage. Carl's hand slaps heavily into the center of my spine, pushing me forward. I stumble on the edge of the rock, unable to generate any forward momentum. I plunge helplessly into the air, arms pinwheeling and legs pumping to gain some balance or control.

I plummet almost straight down, glancing sickeningly off the edge of the rock before tumbling into the freezing water. My arm and shoulder are nearly numb with pain, and I am aware of the warm sensation of blood running down the side if my face in contrast with the chill of the water. I struggle to make my way to the edge, my left arm limp and useless.

As I flounder in the water, I look upward at Carl, still standing at the top of the cliff.

"Pussy," he mutters as he shakes his head, turns and walks away.

SIX

I woke the next morning to a cacophony of snores and other noises filling the dorm. The dim morning light was seeping in around the window curtains and bouncing off of dust motes as they hung lazily in the cool air of the room. I seemed to be the only early riser. A particularly loud snorer was immediately to my left, and I realized with some surprise that it was the petite blonde from Hungary that I'd met the night before. Her tiny stature belied her ability to make a big racket while in slumber mode. I yawned and stretched in my bed, trying to be politely quiet, rubbed the sleep from my eyes and glanced down. I still had my clothes on, including my shoes, but I was covered by an old blanket that I didn't recall pulling over myself. Maybe Blondie had taken pity on me as she was turning in. I folded the blanket back, and got out of bed to tread lightly across the floor and down the stairs toward what I recognized as the aroma of brewing coffee.

Europe has a funny set of attitudes about coffee. There are plenty of powerfully-caffeinated little cups of sludge which will provide you with about two sips and a buzz that will set your ears aquiver, but big cups of steaming java that you can truly savor are harder to find. I followed the scent into the kitchen, where an old-fashioned percolator was perched on the gas stove, pleasantly gurgling away over a blue flame. I pulled a dainty little teacup off a shelf behind the stove and helped myself to as much as it would hold. Early bird gets the worm.

I sat down at a butcher-block table and let the steam from

the coffee drift up over my mustache and nose before taking a sip. Good stuff. I closed my eyes for a second to enjoy the aroma, and when I opened them my hostess was standing in front of me, a concerned look on her face. I gave a little start and wondered how she'd snuck in so quietly. She was a heavy-set, matronly woman, with round shoulders, short legs with thick ankles, and stealth didn't look like her forte. But there she was.

"Good coffee?" she asked, smiling anxiously.

"Yes," I replied, "it's heavenly." She looked slightly confused, and I recalled from the night before that her English was limited. I lifted the cup toward her in a salutary manner and smiled. "Good. *Bien.*"

She nodded, smiling in recognition of my compliment. She wiped her pudgy hands on her flower-print apron and turned to begin the morning preparations for breakfast. Her long brown hair was wound up into an unkempt bun, and her fleshy upper arms jiggled as she cracked eggs into a stainless-steel mixing bowl and whisked them vigorously. I lifted my cup again to her back and silently excused myself to the sitting room at the front of the house.

I pondered my plight as a pickpocket victim. Decisions were easier in the light of day, and I resolved to continue on my journey. This was merely an obstacle, easily overcome. I outlined a plan, beginning with a compilation of debit and credit card contact numbers. I could then locate a bank and see what kind of hoops I would have to jump through to access some cash. In the meantime, the remaining credit card would do for necessary purchases. I had no idea what the credit limit on the card was. I hoped I wouldn't have to find out.

I watched as groggy guests made their way from the sleeping quarters, and I followed them to the big dining room table, where a basic but tasty breakfast of omelets, toast, apple juice and crepes was laid out for the residents. I asked around among the English-speakers about the location of a bank, and a young guy with a black beard wearing tinted glasses said there was one about a block on the other side of the Abbesses Metro station. I asked him about hours of operation, and got a shrug in response.

I retrieved my phone from upstairs and accessed the internet to get numbers for the credit card companies. I needed three, and two of them boasted 24-hour call centers. I waited until most of the other guests had either checked out or embarked on their day in Paris before taking a shower, stowing my gear, putting on clean clothes and letting the hosts know that I would be staying for a couple more days. I wandered out into the bright sunshine in search of a sidewalk café where I could make phone calls in relative privacy.

I didn't have to go far. Sidewalk cafes are as ubiquitous in Paris as beautiful women, and I found one with a bright red awning and wooden tables within a block that fit my needs perfectly. A surprisingly cheerful waitress took my order for a latte, and I started on my calls. The breeze was chilly, but my table in the sun was comfortably warm. I punched in the ridiculously long international numbers and commiserated with the polite representatives at the call centers over my misfortune. Two of them agreed to let me call them back with an address for sending replacement cards, and the third would send a new debit card, but only to my home address as shown on their records. I glanced at the clock on a church tower across the street and decided that it was late enough to call Miranda and accept the Sunday dinner invitation. I could also ask her about using her parents' address as a destination for my new cards. It was Saturday, and both card reps had assured me that they could get the new cards to Paris in no more than three business days.

Miranda seemed pleased to hear from me, and, after gasping appropriately at my tale of woe, was happy to give me her parents' address for mailing purposes. I wrote it down carefully, so that I could give it to the card companies accurately, and jotted down directions to the place for lunch the following day. I thanked her and said that I'd see her then. I finished my latte, tipped the waitress generously and set out to explore my surroundings.

Montmartre is a beautiful part of Paris, off the beaten tourist path, with appeal for both the world traveler and Francophile. The quaint Parisian neighborhoods spill over into commercial areas and tiny parks, eventually dumping out onto Place de Clichy, a gritty section at the bottom of the hill dominated by fast food restaurants, sex shops, strip clubs and the infamous Moulin Rouge.

As I stood in front of Moulin Rouge, I checked my guide-book to verify my suspicion that "moulin" meant "windmill", and noted that there was another "moulin" establishment of note not far away. Curious, I hiked a short distance and located Café des Deux Moulins, which my book informed me was well-known for being featured in a French film. It also told me to expect a long line of tourists, but such was not the case, so I decided to stop in for an early lunch.

I ordered from the Menu de Jour, took my time enjoying smoked herring and studied the movie memorabilia that dominated the décor of the small café. Here's the confusing part: the iconic windmill atop Moulin Rouge is not authentic, it's a reproduction; the Café des Deux Moulins has no actual windmills, but rather is named in honor of the two remaining genuine windmills, which are located nearby, but not visible from the café; there is a restaurant located in the base of one of them, the Moulin Radet, but it is named "Le Moulin de la Gallette", which is actually the name of the other surviving structure. Leave it to the enigmatic French to create mystery out of what seems like the obvious. I lingered over a beer after my relaxed lunch and contemplated the conundrum.

From there, I headed further up the hill that underlies the Montmartre area, atop which is the Basilica of Sacré Coeur, the "Church of the Sacred Heart". This huge jewel that crowns the summit of "the Mount of Martyrs", constructed completely of sparkling white French travertine stone, is absolutely stunning. I watched it become more ominous and more beautiful as I approached, zig-zagging the adjacent streets. By the time I reached the base of the site I was again exhausted and out of breath, so I completed my ascent via the glass-sided funicular that climbs the steepest part of the slope to the base of the church itself. I exited the funicular and walked to the edge of the vast stairway. Paris was, literally, stretched out before my eyes.

The panoramic view from the top of the steps is nothing less than breathtaking. I watched in the warm afternoon sun as hundreds of people gathered on the wide expanse of 270 steps leading up to the entrance of the basilica. Some were spreading out blankets to enjoy picnic lunches, many were taking pictures, and a large group of what appeared to be local youths sang and swayed, accompanied by a guy strumming a guitar. Couples kissed, families squabbled, earnest-looking pilgrims ascended the steps in trance-like states, faces uplifted, and dark-skinned vendors hawked everything from cheap paperweights to bottles of beer. It was a vignette of humanity's diverse nature played out on the world's biggest stage. I was transfixed, and sat watching the constantly-osmosing scene for nearly two hours.

From the steps I went inside the basilica, where I read the welcome notices in four languages. The English version told me not to take pictures or videos, to move along the outer corridors, and to sit only in the pews designated for public seating by thick velvet ropes. The majority of the pews were closed off by black wrought-iron railings. There were vending machines dispensing memorial coins, and wooden boxes with slots on top to accept donations for votive candles, which were piled in boxes alongside.

I sat in one of the demarked pews and watched the exterior light stream through the enormous stained-glass windows, casting pools of luminous color down into several of the alcoves. It was nearly dusk outside by the time I exited through the same huge wooden door by which I had entered.

I ventured around behind the church and made my way down the hill by what I concluded was the "back way", turning around to catch a spectacular view of the white dome of Sacré Coeur at the top of the hill, bathed in the pink and amber-colored light of a Paris sunset.

Further down the slope, I discovered a cozy little square full of genuine French artists, equipped with easels and palettes, and tourists purchasing original works, fresh on the canvases. I watched a family of kids running among the artists, making them nervous. I smiled as their parents, in what sounded like Dutch, scolded them and corralled them into a nearby restaurant booth. Reminiscent of my younger days, as a parent of three, except those scenes had occurred in busy Portland restaurants or the Pike Place Market in Seattle.

It made me think of the earlier email, and I pulled out my phone and sent a short text to my daughter, Lauren, letting her know I was alive, well and in Paris. Given the time difference, it was still very early morning in Portland. She'd see the message when she got up, pass the word along to her brothers, and they'd all be appropriately disinterested.

I spent the rest of the evening with my hostel family. Several of the other guests spoke English, and a couple of them shared my passion for European beers, which we were obligated to sample for purposes of the discussion. The host made a fire in the big hearth in the sitting room, and things got warm and cozy. As the conversation drifted to personal backgrounds, it became apparent that I had accumulated more years of history than almost anyone else in the room, so at their insistence I spent some time describing the American Dream, at least from the perspective of a late-fifties burned-out lawyer. They seemed to find it more interesting than depressing.

I excused myself before it appeared that any of the others

were ready to call it a night, and noticed the blonde Hungarian girl watching me as I departed. She smiled at me, the firelight sparkling in her eyes, but I was in bed and fast asleep before she took up her bunk next to mine, waking me several times as she proceeded to snore the night away.

Sunday morning brought a drizzly, cold rain, more typical for that time of year than the fantastic weather of the previous day. I borrowed an umbrella from the hostel, and set out to see some more of Paris before my luncheon engagement.

I ducked into the cavernous concrete stairway of the Metro station, escaping the rain. I pulled out my map and figured out a route to the Louvre, where I could happily spend the morning out of the inclement weather, enjoying what I'd been told was some pretty good art.

To say the Louvre is overwhelming is a gross under-exaggeration. The general consensus from the guide books is that you should spend two or three days wandering its halls, but I'm not sure even that amount of time could really do it justice. There was something exciting, beautiful or iconic around each corner. It lived up to its reputation as the world's greatest museum.

The *Mona Lisa,* on the other hand, proved to be slightly disappointing. On that particular day there was a crowd of people around the painting at least twenty deep, which I took from comments I overheard to be the case most of the time. It appeared that most viewers settled for raising their phones above the tightly-packed crowd and snapping a picture from a distance. The real surprise for me was the size of the painting. I'd expected it to be a mammoth artwork occupying most of a museum wall, but the portrait of the provocatively smiling lady is little more than twenty by thirty inches, with the visual impression diminished by the fact that you have to view her from so far away, and through a box made of bullet-proof glass. Not to detract from the experience, I'd do it again. I mean, after all, it's the *Mona Lisa.*

SEVEN

The man with the missing finger sorted through the items scattered across the metal table in front of him. The absence of the index finger of his right hand made the process more difficult, but he was growing accustomed to it. His finger had been severed just above the first knuckle, and the flesh that remained was shiny and pink where it had healed. The web of skin on the inside of his thumb was pulled upward into the scar tissue, and it stretched and flexed at the smooth edge of the stump as he manipulated the items on the table top.

"These are mostly credit cards," he said, looking up. "Yes?"

"Yes," came the reply from the man seated across the table from him.

"Have any of these been used for purchases?"

"No. All such cards were destroyed after we used them."

The first man paused thoughtfully. "Were any of those cards used to buy weapons or ammunition?"

The second man hesitated. "Perhaps. But I am not sure."

"Where?"

"In Germany or on the internet, I think. Not here."

"And these?" the first man asked, pointing to a separate pile of items on one corner of the table.

"Identification papers and documents. Passport and travel cards, photo IDs, train passes and such."

"Hmm," the first man said, pushing the pile around with his thumb. He picked up several items, one at a time, scrutinizing them. He looked more closely at one in particular, flipping it over to examine the back. "Hmm," he said again.

"American."

The second man could sense the wheels turning in the first man's head, but he remained silent. He was not involved in planning, decisions or strategy. He was merely a soldier for the cause. He watched as the first man slid the card he had been examining into the pocket of his shirt.

"Burn the rest of these," the first man said firmly. "Not here. Somewhere else."

"I will do so immediately. *As-salāmu 'alaykum.*"

"*As-salāmu 'alaykum.*"

EIGHT

I made it to Miranda's place slightly late. Her parents lived in an attractive brick row house along a beautifully land-scaped street, in a neat and well-cared-for traditional, historic neighborhood. The large yellow flower boxes hanging below the front windows that Miranda had described identified the house for me right away. I spun the little brass knob on the door and a bell rang inside.

The sun-faded blue door was opened by an attractive woman with mahogany-hued hair and dazzling hazel eyes, muted only slightly by that hint of French sadness. A classic *Française* beauty. I quickly introduced myself.

"Of course," she replied in a soft voice, only slightly af-fected by an accent, "we've been expecting you. I'm Cherie, Miranda's mom. Please, come in!" She swung the door wide and motioned with her arm. "May I take your coat and umbrella?"

"Sure," I said, shrugging out of my jacket and leaning the umbrella against the entryway wall. I pulled a bottle of wine from the inside pocket of my jacket as she lifted it from my shoulders. She picked up the umbrella and shook the rain from both items before hanging them from hooks mounted on the high back of an antique bench that dominated one wall of the small space. I looked down and saw both dripping onto the seat of the bench, and she glanced up at me, smiling.

"It's alright," she said, "it has suffered much worse. It's old." My thoughts jumped to people back in the States who would have rushed to prevent water from dripping on a

French antique piece like that. Of course, the house we were in was probably older than my country. Everything is relative.

Cherie was dressed casually, in black athletic pants, a white nylon long-sleeved top, covered by a gray fleece vest with a logo on the left shoulder. Bright yellow running shoes adorned her feet, and it appeared that they were used for their intended purpose, based on her lithe figure. She wasn't necessarily tall, but long-limbed and athletic in appearance. She looked much too young to be Miranda's mother.

"Thanks so much for inviting me. And here..." I said, presenting the bottle of wine to her. "I know absolutely nothing about French wine, other than the fact that I like it. I hope this is okay."

She held the bottle at arm's length to study the label, squinting slightly. "Oh, this will be fine. We'll have it with the meal!" Her smile amped up to about 16,000 kilowatts, and she locked her eyes on mine. Something clicked. I recognized the smile and the energy. So that's where Miranda got it.

"Thank you so much, this is so thoughtful. Come." She took my arm in a firm grip and pulled me around the corner into the kitchen, where Miranda was dutifully chopping some vegetables on a cutting board the size of most dining room tables. Against the large windows at the far end of the room was a dining room table the size of a small car, where Paul was seated.

"Hey, Michael!" Miranda said, waving the knife in my direction. "Welcome."

Paul waggled a hand at me as he studied a newspaper. He looked slightly uncomfortable, making me wonder if things between the parents and the boyfriend had been strained.

A large man lumbered in from the adjacent living room. When I say large, I mean enormous. I'm no midget, at just over six feet and two-hundred ten pounds or so, but this guy made me feel scrawny. I estimated six-feet-six or more, over three-hundred pounds, and generally big, as in beefy, not fat.

He wore a huge pair of dark blue Levi's and a red-and-black checkered shirt, and stood silently at the threshold for several seconds. Visions of Paul Bunyan flashed through my head. Finally, he extended a hand the size of a catcher's mitt toward me.

"I'm Gregor," he said grimly. "Miranda's Pop." I shook the big hand and searched his face for the hint of a smile, but couldn't find one. Unlike his wife, he looked every bit his age, maybe older, his full face lined with creases and folds that only age and stress can produce. His accent was heavily German, and he looked the part; ebony hair, piercing blue eyes, and the physique of an Ardennes draft horse. I half expected him to paw at the floor and snort through his nostrils.

"Nice to meet you," I said, pulling my hand back before he could get a firm grip on it. "Thanks for inviting me."

"All Cherie's doing," he replied dismissively, glancing her direction. I couldn't tell whether it was a rebuff or a compliment aimed at Cherie, but I was beginning to get a feel for the source of Paul's apparent discomfort.

"Pop's a policeman," Miranda chimed in, looking up from her food preparation. "Makes him grumpy. I apologize, you'll get used to it."

Gregor rolled his eyes, took a deep breath, then turned and exited the room, just as he had entered, silently. I responded by raising my eyebrows slightly and trying to keep a pleasant but noncommittal expression on my face. OK, this should be fun.

Dinner actually *was* fun. And delicious. It consisted of a vegetable stew, which Cherie called *potée champenoise*, another dish consisting of several different types of meat in a kind of mashup with duck oil inside a pastry shell, fresh hot bread, and crepes with a rich fruit compote. It was, quite honestly, one of the most delicious meals I'd ever eaten. Miranda dominated the conversation, as was her nature, and Paul was characteristically quiet. Gregor was beyond quiet, way into the silent and sullen spectrum. I sat next to Cherie, and found that we shared a quiet, ironic sense of humor. By the end of dinner, she was elbowing me softly, laughing at things that we both found way more entertaining than anyone else at the table. I caught myself glancing nervously in Gregor's direction to see if he had any objection to this interaction with his spouse, but he seemed to be completely detached from the entire scene, concentrating mainly on the voluminous amounts of food he was consuming.

I asked him, attempting to make some kind of conversation, what sort of policeman he was, but he just looked up from his plate and stared at me. Miranda answered on his behalf, which seemed to be the norm, as he returned to his meal.

"He's a detective with the Prefecture de Police," she said. "A real honor, actually, given that he's a German. They are pretty restrictive in their promotions, but Daddy's really good at solving crimes, I guess. His specialty is murders."

I saw Gregor frown slightly and cast a sideways glance at Miranda, putting an end to that line of conversation. She segued neatly into a history of the French National Police, and their work with the German Federal Ministry of the Interior, where her father had been with the Bundespolizei before coming to France and marrying her mother.

"Michael was pickpocketed, Daddy," Miranda went on after she'd finished her dissertation on European law enforcement. She glanced my way. "Can you do anything to help with that?"

Gregor looked up from his plate impatiently. "Not my department," he replied around a mouthful of food. "Did you lose a pile of Euros?"

"More like a short stack," I replied, holding my fingers up about a half-inch apart. Miranda and Paul tittered, and Gregor narrowed his eyes at me, unsure if I had said something offensive. "Sorry," I went on, "American expression. Not a pile, but enough to be painful."

"Not much anyone can do after the fact," he said, eyeing me warily. "Signs are up all over, warning the tourists, telling them to secure their valuables." He gave me a look which told me he was sure that I had made myself vulnerable to the crime.

"He's right," I said. "It was my fault. I let my guard down, and should have known better." Gregor nodded knowingly, re-focused on his second helping of stew. So much for having an "in" with the Paris police.

Following dinner Paul and Miranda helped Cherie clean up and Gregor exited to the back garden, where he smoked a cigar while standing in the light rain. I ended up remaining at the table, carrying on a scattered conversation with the three as they scurried around the kitchen. I eventually mentioned that I should probably be getting on my way.

"My Pop can run you to the hostel in his car," Miranda volunteered. "He'll be headed home anyway. That way you don't have to walk in the rain." I must have looked confused, which I was, because she went on to explain: "Oh, Mother and Daddy don't live together, haven't for years. No divorce, but 'separated' as you Americans might call it. He comes for Sunday lunch most weeks, especially when I'm home. Very common here." Her tone was matter-of-fact, as if she had explained it a thousand times, but I noticed that Cherie had grown a little uncomfortable.

"Oh, I get it," I said. "Common in the States as well, we're just not quite as civilized about it." Everyone laughed, and I was pleased to see Cherie smiling at me warmly.

Gregor came in from the rain, and Miranda informed him that he would be transporting me, giving him a quick run-down on the hostel location. He grunted in response, grabbed his coat and a battered old hat from the hallway bench, and said: "So come on, then."

I did as he directed, hurriedly thanking Cherie and Miranda on my way out the door, reminding Miranda to let me know when my credit cards came in the mail.

Gregor drove an ancient green Peugeot with rust at the fenders and trash on every surface of the interior. I heard the suspension groan as he lowered himself into the driver's seat. He reached over and swept a jumble of debris from the passenger seat onto the floorboard, and motioned for me to get in.

I expected the drive to be quiet, and it was, other than the rattle and rumble of a dying muffler, which I heard scrape the ground going over several bumps and dips. Either he was adept at navigating through a rain-soaked windshield, or the wipers didn't work. Either way, they never came on during our twenty-minute trek. Neither did the heater. I thanked him as I got out at the hostel and he grunted something in response. I had to admit that it didn't bother me one bit that I would probably never see him again.

I trudged wearily up to the sleeping dorm and laid down for a rest. I was extremely tired for no more than I'd done that day, but I wrote it off to sleeping poorly. A coughing jag which had asserted itself on the chilly drive back to the hostel resumed for several minutes as I lay on my bed, and it left me short of breath. It felt like a chest cold coming on, or bronchitis of some sort, so I fished some Airborne out of my backpack, popped it in my mouth and stretched out on the bed.

The next thing I knew, I awakened to a dark room filled with the now-familiar symphony of snoring. I was, once again, still in my clothes. I kicked off my shoes and pulled up the blanket that someone had again thrown across me. I glanced over to the next bed at the slumbering Hungarian girl, who snorted loudly as she turned over, and thanked her silently.

NINE

My priority the next morning was to get to a bank. I had nearly exhausted my emergency stash of Euros, and I was guarding my remaining U.S. dollars carefully. I put my surviving credit card and my passport protectively into the inside pocket of my jacket and set out to find the financial establishment described to me earlier.

I had to wait thirty minutes for them to open. Fortunately, the weather had warmed up and the sun was shining again, so I waited on a bench in a little square across the street from the bank. I entered as soon as the security guard unlocked the doors. A polite young man in a cheap suit and small green bow tie with a nametag that identified him as "Loeb" came forward to help me when I asked for someone who spoke English.

"*Bonjour, Monsieur*," he said, nodding deferentially to me, "what can I help you with today?"

We worked through the maze of international credit card rules and regulations and settled upon a method whereby I could charge against my card and receive Euros, at a price of course. I didn't care about the fees, one of the realities I had accepted at the beginning of my trip was that it was going to be expensive. Without being stupid about it, I didn't want to waste the entire journey bemoaning how much it was costing. Seemed to defeat the purpose.

He informed me that he would need an address for me in Paris to process the paperwork, and I felt through my pockets for the address Miranda had given me. I read it off to Loeb and he wrote it down. I waited patiently while he interacted with a teller to get my Euros. Forty-five minutes well spent.

I descended into subterranean Paris to negotiate my way on the Metro. The subway cars were much less populated on a weekday morning than they had been on the weekend, but there was still quite a bit of commuter traffic. The scene was almost cliché; there were elderly men in pea coats and berets, middle-aged women in frumpy dresses with long loaves of bread sticking out of their market bags and sharply-dressed business people, both male and female, clad primarily in fashionable black or tones of dark gray, most with scarves of some sort around their necks. Teens with spikey hair and piercings through every conceivable part of their anatomy, people of every description on cell phones or tablets, many with earphones, as well as homeless persons, their meager belongings carefully stowed into bags, strapped onto wheeled carts or piled into backpacks rounded out the travelers, a balance to their more traditional counterparts. The classic and more modern Paris, juxtaposed upon itself. I easily found a seat, and plopped down onto it, catching my breath following my lengthy trip down the stairs.

The Musée d'Orsay was on my agenda for that day, but when I got there, I found it closed. "Shit," I said as I struggled to read the French sign on the door.

"They're pretty much all closed on Mondays. The museums," said a woman behind me in a thick Texas accent, pronouncing the word "meeyuzeeumms". "Sez so in all the guidebooks, darlin'." I turned to look at her, a heavy-set bleached blonde wearing too much makeup, a straw cowboy hat on her head, with a fanny-pack hanging from her considerable waist. Chomping away at a wad of gum, her jowls shaking with each mastication. She reminded me of a constipated dairy cow, anxiously chewing her cud. She also reminded me of what I didn't miss about Americans.

"Thanks," I said, "I'll make note of that." She gave me a bovine stare that evidenced her confusion over whether I had insulted her or not.

My plan to spend the morning with Monet, Manet and Millet thwarted, I wandered toward the river. The Seine flows through the heart of Paris, and is the backbone for most of the tourist destinations in the city; they all seem to be oriented around it. Perhaps that's because the city itself grew up around the waterway, and everything logically became proximate to it. I strolled onto one of the many ornate bridges and watched as a river cruise boat passed below, a few occupants huddled against the cold on the open upper deck.

The water swirled behind the boat as it passed, deep jade in color, cold and powerful. I watched the motion of the current as I admitted to myself that my mood was bleak, that the familiar specter of depression was looming over my shoulder. First time on the trip.

Churchill famously referred to it as his "black dog", an analogy which I found both comforting and familiar. The dark cloud was not an unfamiliar presence for me, I had become used to encountering it unexpectedly and randomly over the years. Medication had helped at various times, but ultimately it boiled down to confronting the thing and wrestling it to the ground. I seldom suffered from long periods of stifling, debilitating ennui which can render many people nearly incapacitated for weeks. For me, they were more like sneak attacks that felt like a fog which dampened the impact of just about everything in my world. Like living life at a diminished speed. And it was usually situational, triggered by the most inconsequential events. It was, however, almost never predictable or convenient. It was what a large part of this trip had been about; a sabbatical from my life aimed at escaping my personal and professional demons. I wasn't sure if it had been working. It wasn't hurting, I knew that with certainty. I leaned against the stone railing of the bridge and stared down into the roiling green water, listening to the faint panting of the black dog, feeling the light pressure as it rubbed against the back of my legs.

TEN

*I*am sitting in courtroom 3A, in Portland's Multnomah County Courthouse. I listen with limited interest as a prosecutor and court-appointed attorney argue the fate of someone who is not in the courtroom, three-year-old Perenzez Harris, my client. "P", as everyone refers to him, was removed from his parents' custody more than a year earlier and placed into foster care while the court and attorneys worked out whether his injuries had been caused by a fall from a bed, as his parents claimed, or at the hand of his father, who was alone in the house with him at the time. Of course, my client is not present, never is. For obvious reasons. Makes my role interesting. They have been grinding away at this particular hearing for almost two hours. A social worker is on the stand, testifying as to the fact that P has been thriving in his foster care environment. The court-appointed attorney for the absent father is trying to elicit an admission from the worker that the boy misses his parents. My role, as court-appointed Guardian Ad Litem for the child, is to make sure his interests are being represented throughout the proceedings. I find my position largely impotent to affect the decisions being made, other than to occasionally state the obvious concern over the child's safety. Thus, my lack of interest. The adults are going to decide this thing, my client is just a quiet cog in the wheel.

Judge James Thompson, a middle-aged, graying jurist with a quick wit, piercing dark eyes and a patient judicial manner, is asking the social worker some additional questions, and I glance at the clock, noting that we are about due *for our midday recess. Judge Thompson's questions are on point, covering several topics of interest. In all likelihood I will, once again, have no questions for the witness, Your Honor. Juvenile Court is different than many other judicial forums in that the Judge takes an active role, rather than serving as a mere referee. Thompson has been at this a long time, and he will be likely to cover anything that the lawyers overlook, which makes us all a little complacent.*

I hear Judge Thompson call the recess and pack up my briefcase. Long morning. Longer afternoon to come. We all suspect where this is headed, and all share the same attitude: just cut to the chase.

ELEVEN

I pulled out my street map of Paris and concluded that I was standing on the Pont Royal Bridge. The map showed that Notre Dame was just a short walk, over another bridge on an island in the middle of the Seine. I decided that it was as good an alternate location as any, stowed my map and set out at an optimistic pace.

The distance looked much shorter on paper than it turned out to be in reality. I was huffing and puffing by the time I reached the mammoth facade of Cathédrale Notre Dame, so the long wait in line to enter came as a welcome respite. It also gave me plenty of time to study the guidebook, and make note of all the images of Saints carved into the huge stone arches that surround the entry portals. I decided my favorite was Saint Denis, depicted holding his own decapitated head in his hands. The story goes that, as the martyred Bishop of Paris, he continued to preach and protest even after he had been beheaded, carrying his severed but still articulate head for ten kilometers before dying. Talk about the perfect patron saint for lawyers.

The interior of the Cathedral is dark and foreboding, and it's not hard to imagine where Victor Hugo drew his inspiration for the tale of Quasimodo. Sure, it's a church, but so much of it is ensconced in historical religious iconography and immense twelfth and thirteenth century architectural features that the actual worship area is a little overshadowed. The one thing that it's hard to say about it is: "a church is a church." This one is unlike most others.

The tour of Notre Dame did nothing to shake my malaise, so I stopped at a café around the corner for a glass of wine and croissant sandwich. It was tasty, but I wasn't all that hungry and the wine did nothing to alter my mood. I located a Metro stop just a half block away and routed myself back to the hostel.

The hike out of the Abbesses station and up the Montmartre hill proved more challenging than ever. I stopped three or four times along the way to catch my breath, self-consciously pretending to look back at the scenery or into a shop window. This was getting old.

Once back at the hostel, even my creaky little bunk seemed like a luscious retreat. I removed my shoes and jacket, laid down, and immediately drifted off into a semi-slumber. There was no one else in the sleeping dorm, and it seemed oddly quiet without the snoring and other noises.

I was vaguely aware of someone entering the room as I snoozed, but it didn't register with my conscious brain until I felt the warm weight of a body next to mine on the narrow bed. Someone had slipped in behind me, someone who smelled faintly of shampoo and cigarettes. I cautiously turned my head to peer over my shoulder and found myself looking directly into the smiling face of my Hungarian bunk neighbor.

"Hello," I said cautiously. "Are you lost?"

She giggled, shaking her blonde hair back from her face. "No, not a bit," she replied. "I was waiting all day for you."

"I see," I said, turning toward her and raising myself up onto an elbow, a maneuver not easily accomplished without knocking her off the bed. It put my face not four inches from hers, our noses nearly touching. "And to what do I owe this honor?"

She gave me a puzzled look, but then grinned and said: "I've been watching you since the other night. I gave you a blanket, you looked so cold." Her accent was heavy, but her English was good. Her pale blue eyes sparkled. She was what I would describe as cute rather than pretty, with roundish features and a full face. Her mop of wavy hair seemed to go every which way, but it had a tousled organization to it. I hadn't noticed before, but I could see from this very close vantage point that she had a spray of tiny freckles across the bridge of her nose. Behind her full lips was a set of crooked, very white, teeth, making for a nice smile. "I have a favor from you," she went on, shifting her weight on the bed so that she could prop an elbow on the mattress and a hand against the side of her head. The hand disappeared into the hair. She wore tight jeans and a cream-colored oversized sweater.

"A favor?" I asked casually. It was hard not to grin back at her, the scenario was so odd as to be almost comical. "OK, shoot. What can I do for you?"

She evidently hadn't rehearsed the conversation beyond that juncture, or maybe she hadn't imagined it would get that far, but she got a little flustered and shy at that point.

"You have good...genes," she said hesitantly. "You are lawyer, yes? Which means you are smart. You are American. And you look like American Nick Nolte, in the films. Yes? With gray hair, but tall and rugged and sexy." She crinkled her face up into what I think was supposed to be a seductive pout. "And I want a baby."

The alarm bells that immediately started going off in my head had to have been audible for several blocks, but she just continued to look at me sweetly.

"Um," I said, shifting my shoulders slightly away from her, "I'm twice your age. I have grown kids. I have zero interest in being a father again. You understand? It's a very nice offer, and I'm flattered believe me, but I think..."

"I am age thirty-two years," she interrupted. "I am no child. I look only for a man with good genes. You will never hear from me about the child." She smiled again; this time I think it was supposed to be reassuring. I found it hard to breathe, and felt a trickle of sweat roll down my back, despite the chilly air in the room.

There are many professional downsides to being an attorney. One of them is to, almost unconsciously, assess the various liabilities present in just about any situation. My lawyer brain was spinning into hyper-drive over this one. I hadn't missed the fact that she had mentioned "American" twice while describing me. The phrases "meal ticket", "paternity proceedings" and "immigration baby" were flashing in brightly-lit neon across my brain. I could still hear the warning bells clanging away. In fact, they had turned into sirens at that point, the European type, with the two-note alternating tones. I realized that her round little breasts were pushing the ribs of her cable-knit sweater to within millimeters of my chest. I glanced up to see her smiling at me, aware of where my eyes had been.

"I think you are interested in my..." she said, searching for the word, "preposition?"

I couldn't help myself, I laughed out loud. She buried her head into my chest, laughing as well.

She threw her head back, shaking her mane of hair again. "The wrong word?"

"Close enough," I said, trying to stifle my laughter. "Close enough." I paused. "Here's the deal...I...I can't do this for you. It's just way too complicated for me to explain. I wish I could, I think you're adorable, but this isn't something I can do. Too many strings..." My voice trailed off. I'd never tried to explain anything like this before.

She turned her face up toward mine, batted her eyes and said casually: "OK, but you can't blame a girl for trying. Correct?" I felt myself exhale, realizing I had been holding my breath.

"I guess not," I said. "And, hey, you can do way better than me."

"No, I don't think so," she said, scowling. "Not here, anyway. Maybe I go to America."

I reached up and flicked a lock of hair from her forehead.

"You are adorable," I repeated. "But I'm not your guy." I shook my head and smiled. "Definitely not your guy."

"OK," she said, rising from the bed. "But I will be right here." She reached across the small space between the beds and patted her empty mattress. "Right here. Your sleeping partner."

"Hooh boy," I said quietly, laying back on the pillow as she turned toward the door. "Hey," I said," What's your name?"

"I am called Ilona," she replied, striking a pixyish pose. "You like?"

"I do. Now, go on and get outta here." I made a shooing motion with my hand. She gave me a faux hurt look and slipped through the door. Suddenly her face reappeared around the edge of the door jamb.

"And you?" she asked. "Your name?"

"Michael."

"Michael," she repeated. She looked thoughtful and smiled. "I like." The face disappeared.

I stared up at the ceiling. I had almost given her another name. The lawyer on duty, protecting me, keeping me at least a little bit anonymous. I'd almost said "Mick." There was truth to it. As a kid, I had detested being called "Mike", so some of the family affectionately referred to me as Mickey. I didn't like that any better. Eventually, I insisted on Michael, and it pretty much stuck. Except for my former wife. From the first time we met, all the way through twenty-seven years of marriage, Patty called me Mick. When introducing me to someone or referring to me in the third person, it was many times Michael. But to my face, when addressing me, in all moods from anger to passion, she almost always called me Mick. In the same way, she was to me, almost always, Patty, even though I occasionally, usually jokingly, called her Patricia.

As if on cue, I felt the phone vibrate in my pocket, and heard the email sound. I pulled it out and looked at the screen, not surprised that it was from her.

"Thanks for touching base with Lauren," it said. "Hope you are OK, take care of yourself."

I hadn't mentioned anything to my daughter in my text about not feeling great. I wondered whether the old spousal intuition was still there after years of being apart, or if she was simply wishing me well. I decided not to give it any further thought, and rolled over onto my side. Just a short nap, that's what I needed. I chuckled to myself as I drifted off, thinking about Ilona and her "preposition". Cute kid. Actually, seven years older than my daughter Lauren, practically a whole decade. Nearly a generation. Would it be so unthinkable? "Hmph," I said to myself. Don't even go there.

TWELVE

The ringtone from my phone woke me up. I was surprised that the room was still light, I'd become so accustomed to waking up in the middle of the night in my clothes. I wrestled the phone out of my pocket and answered.

"Hello Michael, It's Miranda. How are you?"

"I'm good. Did my credit cards arrive?"

"No, not yet. But my mother wanted me to call and invite you to stay at our house, here with us. There is a room and bathroom on the lower level, in the basement, where she thinks you would be much more comfortable than at that hostel. Besides, this is where you will be getting your mail." I could hear the smile in her voice.

I hesitated for maybe a tenth of a second. "Well...thanks," I said. "That would be great! You're sure it's not an imposition?"

"Not at all," she reassured me. "Believe me, my mother wouldn't offer if it would be. She is not inclined to random acts of charity." She paused. "She says you make her laugh." There was a hint of a giggle in her voice. "I know that sounds silly, but she's not laughed much in a long time. You know what I mean?"

"Not really," I said.

The giggling had stopped. Silence ensued. "Just come stay with us, Michael," she said. "It will be a good thing."

"OK," I said, "but I insist on paying something, buying some food or somehow reimbursing her for expenses."

"You can take that up with her," she said, laughing. "Good luck with that." Cherie was evidently more formidable than I had initially realized.

"Alright, let me get my stuff together and head that way. Oh, I'm sorry, is tonight too soon?"

"No, not at all. You'll be just in time for dinner."

"Sounds great, I'll see you in about an hour." I stuck the phone back in my pocket and smiled to myself. A nap, a "preposition" and a stroke of good luck had lifted my dark mood. And I had been spared the temptation of Ilona in the bed next to me, regardless of the ego-booster that had been. All in all, a good afternoon.

After I re-stuffed and organized my backpack, I settled up with the hostel host and headed toward Miranda's. The backpack seemed to have doubled in weight over the last few days, but I wrote it off to a decrease in my endurance from not lugging it around on a full-time basis.

I caught the Metro, headed on a repeat path from Sunday; from the Abbesses station to Pigalle, then switching trains to Blanche and on to Place de Clichy station. In Paris terms, that meant I had traveled from the 18th Arrondissement to the upper corner of the 8th Arrondissement. Rue de Saint-Pétersbourg took me to a side street branching off into a resdential area, where I returned to the now-familiar house midway down the block, on the right side. Home sweet home, complete with yellow window boxes. I paused to catch my breath, then twisted the bell knob.

This time Miranda greeted me, her smile welcoming. "I'm so glad this works out," she said. "It'll be fun having you here. And the neighbors will be abuzz about our American guest. Follow me this way, I'll show you to your room."

We descended a narrow staircase that was accessed by a door off the kitchen, and Miranda pulled a chain that switched on a single bulb in the ceiling. It was clear that the windowless space had been a pantry or cellar at one time, but had been updated to serve as a small bedroom and bathroom. The bath wasn't much, just a toilet, a small sink and a tiny shower stall formed by a plastic curtain on a round rod over a rusted drain in the concrete floor. I, however, was in no position to complain, as this was the Ritz compared to the hostel. And I had it all to myself, no shared accommodations. The bed looked comfortable, and larger than the bunk I'd been sleeping in. I hoisted my backpack onto the bed and surveyed the space.

"This is great, Miranda," I said. "The lap of luxury, by comparison."

She smiled, obviously pleased. "You can come and go as you wish. The door upstairs is just steps from the front door, as you saw, and the other bedrooms are on the upper floors. We won't hear you at all. I'll get you an extra key." She turned toward the stairway. "You can relax and freshen up," she called back over her shoulder, "dinner won't be for an hour. I'll give you a shout."

I sat on the bed and unpacked a few things. I turned on a lamp situated on the small bedside table, which gave the stark space a warm glow. I had really gotten lucky, I acknowledged to myself. This was certainly the best of the accommodations I'd had during the trip, other than a one-night stay at a four-star hotel in Brussels when I'd first arrived. I thought about the fact that they had invited me here, a virtual stranger, without much knowledge of my history or character. You can say what you want about the French being unfriendly, but I didn't know many American families who would be this welcoming to a foreigner without a whole lot of questions, background checks and perhaps security deposits. We can really be a paranoid society. Then again, maybe we have reason to be.

Dinner was, to my surprise, the iconically American Pizza Hut pizza. I guess my initial shock should have been tempered by the knowledge that the U.S.-based company had franchise restaurants worldwide, but it still surprised me. I had actually been hoping for another of Cherie's home-cooked meals. I watched out the kitchen window as the delivery guy motored away on his scooter and smiled to myself. The same, but different. Miranda plopped the familiar boxes, albeit with French wording, onto the table and called out to Paul and her mother that dinner had arrived.

It seemed like a real treat for them, and I decided to share in their enjoyment. We had beer with the pizza, a dark Belgian ale that was the perfect complement to the otherwise pedestrian fare. Paul made a funny toast, and I saw a side of him not evident before, probably the one that had won Miranda's heart. We all sat around the table, exchanging travel stories and comparing various spots in Europe where we had been. Cherie participated vigorously, and it was clear that she was well-traveled, and had encouraged Miranda along the same path. A pleasant evening in a warm and welcoming French home. There's nothing like going native.

At some point during the evening I complimented Cherie on her lovely home.

"Oh, it's my family's home," she said. "Three generations. First my parents lived here, then I grew up here. And I raised my children here. My father died when I was younger, but my mother lived here with us until she passed on. That was, let me see," she looked up and away, calculating silently, "almost six years ago. A very European tradition."

"So, your father built the house originally?" I asked.

"Oh no! He bought it after the war. It had been damaged by the bombings, and he was a... "constuctioneer"? No, a builder, um, a *contractor*." She raised a finger upon finding the right word. "He rebuilt much of it, but the original structure is hundreds of years old."

"Well, it's very nice," I said. For some reason, out of the blue, an image of Gregor, the estranged husband, huddled in some squalid little apartment, exiled from what had been for years his comfortable family home, flashed through my mind. Although I had no reason to wish him ill, I thought to myself that it served him right.

THIRTEEN

*W*e are gathered around a large table in the Child Protective Services offices. There are two attorneys present, me and a guy from the D.A.'s office. The remainder of the seven people seated around the table and elsewhere in the room are social workers and administrators for C.P.S. The topic of discussion is Perenzez Harris. The prior week, Judge Thompson had ordered that he be reintegrated into the household of his biological parents. The evidence of abuse and neglect in the juvenile court case had been too sparse for the court to rule against the parents. P would be transitioned out of his foster home and back to live permanently with his mother and father. None of us think this is a good idea, but none of us can do much about it, other than to plan it in such a way so as to affect P to the smallest degree possible. As if that is even within the realm of possibility.

"They've got an apartment. Two bedrooms, one bath." One of the caseworkers is speaking. "They have been there, oh," she consults her notes, "three and a half months now. No problems, pay the rent on time, utilities stay hooked up. Mom's working at Best Buy, Dad's still looking for a job."

P's parents are both all of eighteen years old. His father, of Asian ancestry, has been involved with gangs and drugs since he was in middle school. His mother, a pretty Hispanic girl, has worked as a stripper, hooker and drug dealer, with P's dad operating as her pimp and supplier. They have never lived together before; in fact, they were practically homeless at the time P came into State custody. They have just recently set up house in an effort to get him back.

"So, can we start off with just some supervised visitation?" another worker asks.

"No," says the first worker, "too restrictive. Remember, the court found no evidence. That really ties our hands."

"And the parents are really pushing," a third worker chimes in. "They want their kid back. Keep pointing out that he's been out of their custody most of his life."

"Maybe that's encouraging," I say. "Maybe they're motivated."

"I think it's more the principle of the thing," the D.A. says solemnly. "You know: 'you've got something that's mine, I want it back'. Fuck."

No one speaks for thirty seconds.

"Let's try some overnights," an administrator says. "See if we can do it in single nights, one at a time, gradually transition to longer periods. Like, wean him away from the foster family. Think the judge will be okay with that?"

"I don't know," one of the workers says, "his last order was: 'make it happen'. He said the kid belonged at home."

It is quiet in the room for a while, and I realize that everyone is looking at me.

"Can you sell it to the judge?" the administrator asks.

"It will carry more weight coming from you," the D.A.'s attorney says. "You represent the kid."

"I can try," I reply hesitantly. "But the judge has had this case on his docket for a long time, and he's ready to be done with it."

The administrator shakes her head in disgust.

"It's not that he doesn't care," I say. "It's just that we've beat this horse to death already, and there's fifty more waiting in line. He wants to move on to one where he might actually be able to do something."

Everyone one in the room nods sullenly and looks anywhere but at me.

FOURTEEN

That night, in the darkness of the basement in my comfortable bed, I had to face a reality. I had not slept well since arriving in Paris. I had written it off to the hostel environment, not the most conducive situation to a good night's rest. But here, in ideal conditions, I was finding that I would wake up almost as soon as I dozed off, either struggling to catch my breath or wheezing in my sleep. I assumed it was the bronchitis that I had developed, but I normally have no trouble sleeping, even with a cold. I tossed and turned for what seemed like an eternity, trying several different positions, using pillows to prop me into an almost sitting posture, to no avail. I eventually gave up and headed to the kitchen for something to drink, or just for a change of surroundings. I filled a glass from the cabinet with water from the tap and sat at the table in the darkness, staring out the window at the quiet street. It had started to rain, and the cobblestones and sidewalks glistened in the meager streetlight.

A noise from the hallway caught my attention, and I saw a light come on up the stairway to the second floor. A minute later, a shadow indicated someone was making their way quietly down the stairs. I did a quick mental once-over of myself to make sure I was decently attired, as I hadn't really expected to encounter anyone in the dead of night. Boxers and a T-shirt, modest enough. I watched the kitchen doorway, and soon Cherie appeared, silhouetted by the dim light behind her. I couldn't help but stare as she paused in the doorway wearing a not-so-long V neck nightshirt made of white jersey fabric, which was all but translucent under the lighting conditions. She clearly wore nothing underneath, and she probably hadn't had any expectation of running into anyone downstairs. I shifted my gaze and made a slight movement in the chair.

"Oh my!" she said softly as she flipped on the kitchen light. "I'm sorry, I didn't know you were there!" Her arms instinctively moved to cover her torso, but her posture was unapologetic and unalarmed.

"No, I'm sorry," I replied. "I shouldn't be up wandering around your house at this hour. I'll take my water and go back downstairs."

"Don't be silly." she said. "Stay right where you are." She turned to the cabinet, pulled out a glass and ran herself some water. She carried it to the table and sat opposite me. "I have the..." I could tell she was searching for the word, "*les insomnie?*"

"Insomnia?" I asked.

"Yes. You have it as well?"

"Not normally, at least not for a long time, but I seem to be having a bout of it lately. I think it's this chest cold I've acquired somewhere along the way, I can't seem to get my breath." We were both talking in hushed tones, leaning toward the center of the table.

"You're having trouble breathing? This can be serious."

"Oh, I think it's more annoying than serious, but I'm going on several nights of it, and I feel a little sleep-deprived."

She made a small clucking noise and reached up to place the back of her hand on my cheek, just below my eye. I resisted the initial urge to pull away. Her hand was soft and warm on my face. "No fever, I think," she observed. Her hand lingered. I didn't mind. "Oh, I'm sorry. You wouldn't know. I am trained as a nurse." She pulled her hand away. "I do things without thinking."

"No, no, that's fine. I don't mind at all. I didn't realize that you worked."

"I don't anymore. Or right now, I guess. My *clinique* closed last year, the physician retired. I have not really looked hard for a new job; I enjoy my freedom." She smiled, and tiny lines appeared at the corners of her eyes, along with a set of shallow parentheses on either side of her mouth. "I have noticed your cough. Pneumonia is, of course, a concern." She studied my face carefully. I couldn't tell if it was diagnostic or otherwise.

"I think I would know if I had pneumonia," I said, taking a sip of water. My throat was a little dry. As if on cue, the swallow triggered a cough, and I instinctively covered my mouth with the crook of my arm.

"You don't always know. There is *le marché pneumonie*, the walking pneumonia. People are not always aware." She paused, still studying my face. "I can get you in to see a physician, one that I know."

"Thanks, I appreciate it, but I think I'll see how I do over the next few days, especially now that I have very nice sleeping accommodations, thanks to you."

"As you wish," she said, still smiling. "So, as we are both awake, tell me more about yourself."

I shrugged and looked away. "I'm not sure what you would want to know..."

"All," she replied succinctly.

I was completely taken in by her honest interest, her disarming manner, and her unabashed disregard for the fact that I could clearly see the contours of her very nice breasts beneath the flimsy fabric of the nightshirt. Did I mention that it was chilly in the room? So, I talked.

Fact of the matter was, we both talked. The conversation eventually went back and forth, as we both asked questions and took segues down seemingly uninteresting paths, only to discover some parallel in the other's dialog that bound them together in some way. She was witty, intelligent, curious and charming, with a delicious, infectious laugh. She got up several times to get us more water, some tissues, and a snack of English biscuits, and I was treated to glimpses of her bare and very shapely bottom as she reached up into the cabinets. She clearly didn't care. We laughed until our sides hurt, quieting ourselves several times as the volume got above a loud whisper. We leaned forward and listened to each other intently. We reached across the table and clutched each other's hands, tapping one another's forearms to emphasize a point.

As we talked and laughed well into the wee hours, I was shocked to feel the stirring of some feelings in my chest. I know full well that our "hearts", our emotional centers, are located somewhere in the grey matter of our brains. But somehow, we sense strong emotions from some physical point in our chest or our gut, which gave rise, I suppose, to the ancient belief that our emotional centers were headquartered in our hearts. This woman, this attractive, exciting, radiant creature before me, was triggering feelings I'd not had in years, if ever. It thrilled me and scared me to death, simultaneously. I couldn't control it, just roll with it as it washed over me, trying to enjoy it for what it was. Whatever it was.

The conversation carried well into morning, and I saw the first glimmer of daylight outside the window.

"Would you like some coffee?" she asked, noticing the nascent light outside as well.

"American-style coffee, brewed, in a mug?" I asked.

"I have a Keurig machine," she said. "Starbucks K-cups, if you like."

I grinned so broadly it hurt my face a little. "You, Cherie, are a woman after my heart."

She stood and smiled coyly, not responding. "Coffee," she said, "coming up."

I sat back comfortably in my chair as she prepared the Keurig machine, exhausted but feeling better than I had for days. The sleep deprivation and the black dog had retreated into a corner, biding their time, but out of the picture for the moment. I closed my eyes, happily waiting for the delicious aroma of the coffee to fill the room.

Both of us turned as we heard footsteps on the stairs. Miranda shuffled into the doorway, her long, dark hair in a tangled mass that surrounded her face and fell haphazardly over her shoulders, wearing a flannel nightgown in a faded blue print that tumbled down over the tops of the fluffy pink slippers on her feet.

"You two are up early," she said, rubbing one eye with the back of her hand. She wandered to the refrigerator, pulling the door open. She stared into the interior for several seconds, then dragged out a bottle of orange juice, carrying it to the counter and grabbing a glass from the cabinet above. The refrigerator door was still open, hanging out into the middle of the room. Miranda slumped against the cabinet and drank thirstily from the glass of juice and sighed, clearly not intending to return the bottle of juice or close the door. Kids are the same, the world over. She glanced in Cherie's direction and groaned quietly to herself.

"Mother," she said with exasperation, "some underwear, please? We have houseguests."

"It is my house, they are my guests," Cherie replied, slipping me a conspiratorial grin. "I will dress as I please."

"No complaints from me." No, I didn't say it. But I definitely thought it. Miranda just shook her head as she placed her empty glass into the sink. She wiped her hands on the front of her nightgown and walked over to occupy the chair opposite me at the table.

"Coffee, dear?" Cherie asked Miranda, a sweet note in her voice.

"Yuck," Miranda said, making an awful face. "You know I hate coffee."

"Just trying to be a good host, dear." Cherie was enjoying this. I have to admit, I was too.

Cherie delivered my coffee in a big, white porcelain mug,

like you might find in a classic American diner, steaming and fresh from the Keurig. "Starbucks breakfast blend, as promised," she said. She patted the back of my hand as I took the mug from her.

"So, what is your plan today, Michael?" Miranda asked as she pulled a stray strand of hair from the corner of her mouth.

"I thought I would go to Versailles. I think I can get all the way there on the train."

Miranda nodded thoughtfully. "Yes, I think so. I haven't been there since I was a kid. I was unimpressed." She shrugged apologetically, raising her eyebrows slightly. "Long train ride."

"Well, it's one of the sights us Americans have to see. Everyone always asks: 'Did you go to the Eiffel Tower? Did you see Versailles?' It's kind of mandatory for us."

"I understand," she said. "The Statue of Liberty is probably not so big a deal if you live in New York City."

"Something like that," I said. "Anyway, that's all I have on my agenda for the day. Anyone want to tag along?" It was a transparent invitation aimed at Cherie, but Miranda didn't pick up on that.

"No," she replied, "Paul and I have some things to arrange before I head back to school. Classes start back up Thursday." Her mother busied herself with the Keurig and didn't respond.

FIFTEEN

A group of nine men prepared in near silence, with only an occasional hushed inquiry and grunted response. They were nearly uniform in their physical appearance; most were young, had dark beards or facial hair, dark eyes and skin, and were medium to slight in stature.

The man with the missing finger was the exception. He was clean-shaven, and more robust; well over six feet tall, barrel-chested and rooted firmly on legs that looked like tree trunks. The thickness of his body was accentuated by the black Kevlar vest he wore, strapped into place by nylon Velcro straps. His baggy black pants had cargo pockets up and down the outer seams, all the way to the hem at his ankle. He was older than the others, by perhaps eight or ten years. He was clearly in charge, and they were all deferential toward him.

He walked around the room, watching the other men closely as they went about their preparations. Most were donning outfits identical to his, and several who were already dressed were loading weapons on a long table against one wall of the room. Semi-automatic and automatic rifles of several types were lined up side-by-side, barrels pointing toward the wall. Handguns were similarly aligned, most of them black semi-automatics; Glocks. Berettas or Sig Sauers. Each pistol had several full magazines neatly stacked next to the handgrips. At the far end of the table were more handguns, these revolvers, mostly chrome and stainless steel, and an assortment of grenades and other explosive devices, including what looked like a few sticks of dynamite and some gray putty wrapped in clear cellophane. Almost every man also had a large knife in a sheath strapped to the outside of his leg.

"We are no longer in the planning stages," said the large man, breaking the silence. "The time has come for us to rain death on the infidels." He paused, looking back and forth among the other men's faces. "It is time for us to bring *jihad* against the blasphemers of *Allah*."

The men stirred in the resulting silence.

"*Jihad*," muttered one of them cautiously.

"*Jihad*," several repeated after him. Then more of them, again: "*Jihad*!"

"Against the infidels!" piped up another voice, louder and with more confidence. "Death to the infidels!"

"Death to the infidels!" came a chorus of voices in response. "Death to the infidels!"

The man with the missing finger looked around the room, pausing to stare briefly into the eyes of each of the other men. The air in the room was dank and fetid, the tension palpable. "You are ready," he said firmly. "*Allahu Akbar!*"

"*Allahu Akbar!*" came the unanimous response, in a roar that rattled the windows of the small room.

SIXTEEN

Cherie treated us to a delicious breakfast of spiced eggs and hot rolls with cheese sauce, then excused herself to her room upstairs. I had trouble reading her mood, but I didn't feel that the magic of the night before was lost. She got firm with me during breakfast when I tried to insist that I make some sort of payment or buy some food while I was there, dismissively saying that "such nonsense" was "out of the question". She was playful about it without leaving any doubt that it was a closed subject. Miranda shot me an "I told you so" look with a smile.

I helped Miranda clean up and wash the dishes while Paul scrounged around to salvage some of what had been left uneaten. He had slept through most of our breakfast, coming down as Cherie was going up.

After the cleanup, I headed down to my room and pulled out my Metro map, charting a course to Versailles. It looked like a fairly long trip, and I was hoping to take another shot at Musée d'Orsay in the afternoon. I got dressed, loaded up my pockets, picked up the house key that Miranda had given me, and headed out. The kitchen was abandoned as I passed through, so I bid everyone a good day silently in my head.

In the Place de Clichy station, I paused for a brief musical interlude provided by a scruffy kid deep in one of the subway passages playing a 12-string guitar with mastery beyond his years. He launched into a spirited rendition of "Classical Gas" that was amazing. I dropped five Euros into his battered guitar case and applauded, along with about a dozen others.

With the uplifting music still humming in my head, I was on my way by 8:30.

Miranda had been correct, it was a long, challenging trip via the Metro and train. But the people-watching was fabulous. Such a mixed bag of characters and everyday folks, certainly like few other places in the world. Between the scenery, navigating with my map and watching the rolling show of human diversity, the trip went quickly.

Château de Versailles didn't disappoint. It was every bit as opulent, lavish, ridiculous and over-the-top as I had expected. The French royalty in the seventeenth and eighteenth centuries certainly knew how to put on a show of wealth and power. A long succession of guys named Louis made a point of rubbing it in the face of anyone willing to look that they had more money than sense, until the French people finally had enough of it and revolted, giving us Americans a very entertaining play and movie. The monument to all that excess, however, still stands to remind us, or perhaps warn us, that absolute power corrupts absolutely (credit as due to Lord Acton).

The tour was fascinating, but it wore me out, and I was looking forward to the return time on the train to rest. I grabbed lunch in a nearby cafe before boarding. Full and sleepy, I found a seat and settled in for the trip.

Two minutes into the first leg of the trek it was clear that something was up. There was an electrical buzz among the passengers. Short, hushed conversations, wide-eyed responses, and muted expressions of incredulity scattered among the various people in my car. Many were looking at, and sharing with each other, their phone screens. My inability to understand, or for the most part even hear, the conversations didn't hamper my interpretation of their seriousness. People were concerned and surprised. My instincts were confirmed when, at the first stop we reached, a gendarme armed with a sleek black automatic weapon stepped into our car, grim-faced and intent, and surveyed the passengers. This was not your traditional French policeman, in the blue uniform, riding boots, buttoned-up cape and funny brimmed cap. This guy was in full black battle gear, including Kevlar vest and riot helmet. I could see out the window that the same thing was occurring simultaneously in the other cars, up and down the train, and that there were more traditionally-uniformed patrol officers standing alertly on the platform. This was not standard procedure, or at least hadn't been during the time I had been traveling around Paris.

I instinctively sat still, trying to look calm and innocent. Of what, I wasn't sure, but I noticed many around me doing the same thing. Some stared openly at the officer, but most just gazed off into the middle distance, ignoring him. After his completed review, he stepped back through the doors onto the platform, continuing to scan the car as the doors slid shut and the train moved out. It was quiet in the car until we had traveled maybe half a mile, and then the whispered conversations began again.

I was just about to ask the woman next to me if she spoke English, and make an inquiry as to what was going on, when my phone rang. I pulled it out of my pocket and glanced at the caller ID. It was Miranda.

"Hi, Miranda," I answered.

There was a short pause, and then I heard Cherie's voice: "Oh, this is Cherie, I'm using Miranda's phone."

"Oh, hi, Cherie. It's good to hear from you."

"Well, not so good, I'm afraid. There are some policemen here, looking for you. They are going through your things, downstairs. They want to know where to find you."

"I'm on the train," I responded. "They want to speak to me? Specifically? They asked for me by name?"

"Yes."

I thought for second. "Tell them I'm on my way back there. I should be there in, say, forty-five minutes."

There was a muffled conversation, and then she came back

on the line. "That is not acceptable, they want to know what train you are on, and where."

I looked out the window, thinking. "That doesn't work for me," I said, my mind racing. "I'll be there in forty-five minutes."

"Oh," she said with surprise. "I will...I will tell them. And I have called Gregor..."

I hung up before I could hear any more, afraid that someone more insistent might get on the line. I shut down my phone completely, then shoved it into my pocket. So much for my plans to visit the d'Orsay. That destination seemed to be jinxed.

The remainder of the trip was tense. The gendarmes continued to board at each stop, and were a presence in every station. None of them, however, took a particular interest in me as I made the connections toward Cherie's place. Could it be possible that the two things were related? Could this comprehensive effort be aimed at locating me? If so, it wasn't working very well. Several of them had looked me right in the eye as they boarded, without a flicker of recognition. I scoured my mind for some reason that the authorities would be looking for me. The thought occurred to me that someone back in the States might be trying to notify me of an emergency, but I couldn't figure out why they wouldn't just call my phone. By then I had become too paranoid to ask anyone else on the train what was going on, for fear they would recognize me and turn me in. Turn me in for what? That question banged away on my brain like a sledgehammer.

SEVENTEEN

*I*t is 1983, and I am sitting in a large classroom on the University of Oregon campus taking the Oregon State Bar Examination when I am struck by a sudden concern. It's not what you might think, I am not worried that I won't pass the Bar, I am confident that I will. My concern is over the fact that I don't really want to be a lawyer. A strange thought to have in the middle of the exam, after three years of studying the law.

I have arrived here naturally; my father and his father before him were lawyers. I took a direct collegiate course of study, pre-law all the way. My grades have always been good. I have all the right business and political connections to make a fine career out of practicing law. I have exhibited the characteristics that will make me a decent advocate, counselor and negotiator. My mind is relatively quick and nimble, able to soak up facts, and to recall them with respectable speed, upon demand.

But my heart seems to be in a different place. Despite the adrenaline-rush of doing battle upon a field if wits, and the remuneration that comes with it, I find myself wondering what good I will be accomplishing by exercising my legal muscle. My father and grandfather have spent many years between them building a very respected and successful legal practice, and they are known for their professionalism and expertise in the law. They have told me that I possess all of the qualities necessary to carry on that tradition, and that they will be more than thrilled to see that happen. I'm not so sure.

I've never embraced the right-brain, left-brain thing, feeling like an anomaly when the discussion comes up. In my own self-analysis, I seem to be both. And the combination of opposing characteristics creates a strange juxtaposition of skills, talents, ideas and desires that are constantly at war in my head and my heart.

My personal relationships have been clouded by this enigma as well. At the age of twenty-five, I have dated several women for extended periods of time, but eventually the relationships have all failed. It is not because either of us are bad mates or matches. We always seem to get along quite well. But at some juncture in the journey, I am struck by the feeling that I am withholding something, that I am incapable of total commitment to another person. I have never related, in any way, to the expression "head over heels". It just doesn't happen to me. As in my educational and professional endeavors, I enter my closest personal relationships with the understanding that they can never really be all "good" or all "bad". They will always be somewhere in between. Mine is a world of gray, with virtually no black or white. That seems to be my talent; avoiding the extremes to remain safely on the middle track, using my skills to weave just slightly on either side of the proverbial center line, staying securely within the inner lanes.

My musings are interrupted by an announcement from the exam proctor that there are only thirty minutes remaining. I hunch over, pencil in hand, to focus on the task before me. One thing at a time.

EIGHTEEN

My feet felt like they had lead weights on them as I walked from the Metro station to Cherie's house. I didn't know what to expect, but I was surprised at the fact that there were only two cars in front of the house; a black BMW that I suspected was the police vehicle, and Gregor's Peugeot. That fact made it even harder to imagine any sort of link between me and the police activity at the train stations.

I could barely catch my breath as I ascended the stairs to the front stoop, wondering if I should ring, or just go in with my key. I decided to maintain as much separation as I could for the sake of my host, and rang the bell.

Gregor swung the door open as soon as I let go of the ringer, filling the doorway with his mass. He had on light green polyester slacks that were challenged by his girth, a white shirt, print tie hanging loosely from his collar that didn't make it halfway over his belly, and a tan tweed sport coat that could have easily been used as a circus tent. Not exactly a fashion statement, but he looked more like a policeman than he had the previous Sunday. I could see Cherie hovering in the hallway, catching her eye briefly.

"Bad move," Gregor said, "putting them off like that. They are not pleased." I took it that the policemen inside were not a part of his department, or maybe even his force.

"Sorry," I said. "Habit and training, I guess. Give yourself time to think. Not that I had anything to think about..."

"Get on in here, let's get this done. See what the big mystery is about."

"They haven't told you?"

"Not a word. Do you want to tell me?" Typical cop tactic.

"Nothing to tell," I said, moving past him into the kitchen.

Seated on one side of the table were two men in dark suits with muted ties, looking at me with annoyance. They both had neatly-cropped hair, not quite military, but regulated in appearance. The older of the two, probably in his late forties, with some gray in his hair, looked especially annoyed.

"Monsieur McCann," he said curtly, without rising from his chair. "Have a seat." He pointed at a chair opposite the two of them. "If you don't mind." The sarcasm wasn't lost on me. I sat.

"First of all, let me say that you should have let us know your location and we could have brought you in," he said immediately. His English was good, only slightly accented. I was guessing national government or diplomatic service. "We have a few questions for you. I understand that you are an attorney by trade in the U.S.?"

"I am."

"Please keep in mind that we are not in the U.S. Many of your laws and rules do not apply here."

"I'm well aware of that."

"Good, then. We will proceed. What do you know of *Charlie Hebdo*?" The question caught me completely at a loss, but I sensed some sort of reaction from Gregor, who was standing at the far end of the room.

"Nothing," I said levelly. "I don't know who that is." The younger of the two glanced at his partner.

"So, *Charlie Hebdo* means nothing to you," the spokesman went on.

"Nothing."

"Where have you been today?"

"Tourist stuff. Mostly to and from Versailles."

"Alone?"

"Except for the other tourists and commuters on the trains."

"So not with anyone you know?"

"By that do you mean anyone who can vouch for my whereabouts?"

"Yes."

"Then, no."

The two men looked at each other. The elder one nodded.

"Well, then," the younger one said, speaking for the first time. "We will need you to come with us." I didn't like the fact that he placed my passport on the table in front of him as he spoke. I liked it even less when he slipped it into the pocket of his jacket.

"Hold on just a minute," I said. "I know this isn't America, and I don't have all the nice Constitutional rights I'm used to there, but I think I'm entitled to some basic information." I glanced at Gregor, hoping for some support. His face showed nothing. "Who are you guys, and where are you proposing to take me?"

Both men stared at me, silently. Older guy finally reached into his suit coat and pulled out a worn leather wallet. He opened it, laid it flat on the table and spun it around so that I could see the I.D. behind the protective plastic. "We are from the Terrorism Brigade," he said flatly.

NINETEEN

It *is nine o'clock on a Thursday evening, and I have on worn jeans, sneakers and an old sweatshirt with a faded duck on the front of it. I am sitting at a Formica-topped table in a small, plain conference room in the Portland Police Department headquarters with a uniformed officer, two detectives and two social workers, both women, both dressed as if they had been relaxing at home with their families, watching television. One of the social workers has been crying, and is wiping her eyes with a tissue. The other worker has her arm around her. One of the detectives, wearing khakis and a green polo shirt with a brown leather shoulder holster strapped over it, is doing the talking.*

"Officer Randall was called to the residence at approximately 5:15 p.m.," he says, nodding toward the uniformed officer. "A neighbor called it in. Said they heard the child crying and crying, and then nothing. Thought it was odd."

"Been there before," officer Randall volunteers. "Several times." He looks down, adjusting his service belt, pulling at the front of his shirt. Uncomfortable. The detective looks at him, waiting. When the officer remains silent, the detective picks up the narrative.

"Randall found the child inside the residence, unresponsive and visibly injured. Adult male was in the room, passed out on the sofa. Randall called in the EMTs and backup. Then he had the dispatcher notify Child Protective Services." He nods toward the two social workers. "They met the bus at Legacy Good Samaritan. Evidently, they called you."

The detective is responding to my request to be filled in on what had happened earlier in the evening. The social workers are looking at me expectantly, wanting me to do something. I understand their expectations, and their anxiety. I also understand that there is nothing I can do.

"How is P?" I ask the workers.

The one who is not crying, a large, black, middle-aged woman, says: "He's a fighter. He's hangin' in there." My recollection is that her name is Mary. I nod at her, and she tightens her grip around the shoulder of the other worker, like a big mama bear.

"Medically, what's the status?"

The other detective, this one in a pale gray suit and yellow tie, clears his throat. "Medical report is that the child, a Perenzez Harris, has a fractured skull and ribs, lacerations to the liver and lungs, and a spinal cord hemorrhage," he says. The other social worker, a young white girl with long brown hair and big glasses who looks like she could still be in high school, sobs loudly. I don't recall her name. "Condition is..." the detective hesitates, "Condition is critical."

"Adult male is in custody," the first detective goes on. "He came around on the ride in. Looks like a tweaker. Says he's the kid's dad."

"Officer Randall, you said you'd been there before." I say. "Why?"

Randall continues to look uncomfortable, probably concerned about some blame blowing back on him.

"Noise," he replies. "Partying. Suspected substances. No violence."

I nod and look down, staring at my hands, fighting back some tears of my own. "Guess there's not much more we can do," I say. "Maybe pray for P, if you are so inclined." Everyone else just nods.

TWENTY

Gregor and I rode in the back seat of the BMW, with the two suits in front. It was a black-on-black 5-series, with darkly tinted windows. No visible police lighting, no extra antennas. They didn't put me in handcuffs or treat me like I was being arrested, and had no objection when Cherie suggested that Gregor accompany me. He didn't seem very eager, but came along just the same. The younger guy was an excellent driver, maneuvering through traffic, pushing the motor hard. The ride was completely silent, except for road sounds and the ambient noise of the city, no police radio chatter or conversation between the occupants. After about thirty minutes, we arrived at a big stone building surrounded by a tall iron fence with spikes at the top. We drove through a mechanized gate in the fence that swung open as we approached, and pulled down a steep concrete ramp into an underground parking garage.

From the car, we walked through the garage to an elevator, which we rode to the third floor of the building, where the two suits and Gregor exchanged some words in French. We wound our way down several hallways to a small room with a table around which were several wooden chairs. The suits ushered me, along with Gregor, into the room. They conversed with him quietly, and then left us there, closing the door behind them.

"What's happening?" I asked him after they were gone.

"They are not telling me anything," he said. "They are coming back to question you further."

"Who the hell is Charlie Hebdo?" I asked him. "You reacted when they mentioned the name."

He looked at me silently for several seconds. "You really were on the train and at the palace all morning, weren't you?" he said, as if it had finally sunk in.

"I certainly was!" I responded emphatically. "I have no reason to lie to these people, or to you. Now, who the hell is Charlie Hebdo?"

At that moment, the door to the room opened and a tall, gray-haired man in a white dress shirt with the sleeves turned up and a loosened blue tie walked in, carrying a file. He was thin, in a non-fit, French way, and had an air of authority about him that seemed to fill the room. He had a large beak nose that dominated his face, thick black eyebrows, dark circles under his eyes and what looked like a permanent five-o'clock shadow across the lower part of his face. His expression was drawn and serious. He made eye contact with Gregor and motioned with his head for him to exit the room. Gregor said something to him in French, looked at me, and walked out, closing the door as he left. The man motioned me toward the table, saying: "Please, sit."

I took a seat in one of the wooden chairs, and he sat across from me. "I am Chief Malboeuf," he said, opening and examining the file in his hands. His long, slender fingers cradled the folder almost delicately. "I apologize for any inconvenience we may have caused you, but these are matters of utmost importance. We appreciate your cooperation." His English was close to perfect, nearly unaccented.

"I wasn't really given much choice."

He looked up at me, an expression of surprise on his face. "I am sorry if it seemed that way to you, but you are here on a strictly voluntary basis. I thought that was clear."

The hell it was, but I thought that a battle best left unfought. "Chief, I would just like to know what is going on and why I am here."

Malboeuf took a deep breath and exhaled. He was

thoughtful, pulling at the knot of his tie. "We have had..." he started and then stopped. "We have had a terrible thing happen in our city." He glanced at his watch. "This morning, less than four hours ago, there was a terrorist attack. People have died, and the terrorists, as we speak, are still at large."

I sat back in my chair, taking in the information. I realized that my lungs had the same feeling that I had experienced during the last few nights; not enough air. I tried to gather my thoughts, and breathe.

"I'm still not sure what any of this has to do with me," I said, trying to regain my composure.

I could tell Malboeuf was deliberating over something. He moved the file back and forth in his hands, looking at me in a scrutinizing way. "A newspaper's offices were raided and several of the staff members were killed. The name of the paper, really more of a magazine, is *Charlie Hebdo*. They publish politically antagonistic material and drawings."

I was processing things. The police activity on the trains and subways made sense. "But how does any of that," I asked, "involve me?"

Malboeuf opened the file and glanced down at it. He removed a piece of paper, turning it toward me, pushing it across the table.

I looked at the paper, a back-and-white photocopy, trying to make sense of it. The familiar image in a blurry, enlarged, unfamiliar context finally registered with me. On it was my face.

"That's a copy of my driver's license," I said. I could see that the word "Oregon" at the top and a portion of the State seal were obliterated by a dark gray smear. I pointed to the smear. "What's that?"

"Blood," he replied. "This was found at the scene of the attack."

My head was reeling with a thousand thoughts and nearly as many questions. "You said 'at the scene'. What does that mean?"

He pointed at the dark discoloration on the paper. "That is, presumably, a victim's blood on the license. It was found inside the offices."

I didn't know what to say. I just sat there, stunned, staring at the image on the paper.

"I think you can see why we felt it was necessary to speak with you." Malboeuf said as he pulled the paper back and returned it to the file. "We will have more questions for you, but for now we will be holding you here. Consider it a detention, not an incarceration. You will have the opportunity to contact your embassy at a later juncture, if you desire."

"But I was pickpocketed," I protested weakly. "My license, it was stolen. It was in my wallet, along with my money."

Malboeuf picked up his file and stood. "We are aware of that," he said. "We are also aware that you have been Detective Wolfert's guest. We are taking those things into consideration."

Unfortunately, I understood exactly where he was coming from. Until they'd had a chance to let the dust settle, sort out the facts, get some further information, it made sense for them to question and hold me. He had said that it hadn't even been four hours since the attack. I was fortunate that they hadn't shot me on sight. I watched helplessly as he left the room and closed the door.

Gregor was escorted back into the room by one of the suits that brought us. "They are telling me that you are going to be staying," he said. "I need to leave; I have work to do."

"Wait," I said. "I have a few questions."

"I am not sure I have any answers for you."

"Well, let's start with how they knew where to find me."

"Evidently, you gave Cherie's address while you were doing a money transaction. The first thing they looked for once they had your name was financial activity."

Of course. That made sense. I got onto the grid through the bank. Big brother was watching.

"Can you help me out here, Gregor?" I asked.

He pulled at his weathered face, rubbed the back of his neck. "This is above my level. This is National Police. I'm just a local detective. I have no influence."

"Come on, I know how cops work. They'll listen to you."

"But what can I tell them? I don't really know you. We had lunch. My daughter dragged you home from Bonn. I'm not going out on a limb."

"But you told them about the pickpocket incident. You told them I was your guest."

He looked uncomfortable. He shifted his considerable weight, avoided eye contact with me, studying the tops of his shoes. "Cherie told them all that, while they were at the house."

Oh. That was different.

He looked up. "And you're *schtupping* my wife," he said, with sudden vigor. "Why should I want to help you?"

"I'm, no. I'm..." I started to protest. Yiddish from a German. I have to admit, it threw me a bit off balance.

"Or at least you're trying to," he went on. "I don't blame you, she's a beautiful woman." He paused, his bluster fading. Evidently, Gregor was more observant than he let on, probably a good quality in a cop. "I could never make her happy." He caught my furtive glance. "Oh, not like that. Love and affection, that kind of stuff. I'm not good at."

"I'm sorry you think that of me, Gregor," I said, recovering a little. "It's not true, by the way. But don't you think that's a minor thing, here in my circumstances?"

He looked at me, his countenance still slightly stormy. "As I said, I have my own work to do." He turned and knocked on the closed door. It opened and the suit let him out.

"Excuse me," I said before the door could shut. "Am I going to be 'detained' in this room? Do I have access to restroom facilities?"

The guy looked at me like he didn't understand. Funny, his English had been good back at the house, when they were questioning me.

"Toilette?" I asked, trying to simplify things. He motioned for me to follow, and pointed at a door across the hallway.

"Make it fast," he said, "or I will have to come in for you." Talk about performance anxiety.

TWENTY-ONE

After thirty minutes back in the room, it was apparent that I *would* be waiting there. I strolled over to the window and looked out. There were bars on the outside of the glass, but the view, all things being considered, wasn't too shabby; a slice of downtown Paris that looked like the front of a post-card. They hadn't confiscated my personal belongings or my shoelaces, so I pulled out my phone to check the signal and charge. I only had about 20% battery left, which I decided to conserve, given that I had no idea how long I would be there. I sat back at the table, pulled one of the chairs over to rest my feet on, and contemplated my dilemma. Not much else for me to do. I thought about whether I should call someone while I had the opportunity. No one came to mind.

After half an hour a different guy in a dark suit, this one younger than the other two, entered the room, trailed by a secretarial-looking young woman carrying a stenographer's pad. Both sat at the table with me. The guy's tie was bright red, much bolder than his buddies'. He also had neatly-trimmed hair, but it was longer than the others. Generational differences, I was guessing. The secretary had on a no-nonsense navy skirt, white blouse and practical, flat shoes. Her brown hair was cropped short, just below her ears, where her ear-rings dangled out from under. She wore no rings or nail polish on her slender fingers. Just a hint of lipstick.

"Monsieur McCann," the young man began. "I am here to get some more detailed information from you." His English wasn't great, but was good enough to ask questions. He didn't introduce himself or the young lady. She opened the pad, crossed her legs and sat back in her chair; pen poised.

"Okay," I said, "what do you want to know?"

"Let us start with the pickpocket incident. Give all the details."

I proceeded to do so, in probably more detail than he wanted, but what the hell, I had nowhere else to go. We moved on to a similarly detailed account of my whereabouts and activities during the morning. The secretary scribbled away on her pad in shorthand, evidently having no problem keeping up. I wondered if they were recording the entire session as well, but I admired her mastery of a lost art, especially since I assumed that she was transcribing a foreign language.

We expanded the narrative to include my goings-on since I had reached Paris, and even my connection with Paul and Miranda in Bonn, by way of explaining how I had ended up there. I didn't include my encounter with Ilona, although I did consider it, just for grins.

He asked for a detailed inventory of the contents of my wallet. In addition to the credit cards and insurance identifiers, he pressed me for details on things like club memberships and personal papers. He especially emphasized the issue of my passport, and whether there were any links to that information in the wallet. I didn't think so.

We finished the session, and the pair left without fanfare, giving me no indication of what my immediate future looked like.

At around five o'clock the suit that had been minding the door and a uniformed gendarme escorted me down a couple floors to an actual holding facility. This time they took my personal items, but not my shoelaces. I made sure to turn off my phone so it would have at least a little battery left when I got it back. I signed the inventory for my stuff and they left me alone in my new room. This one had a smaller window; high up in the gray wall, bars on the inside, no view. A basic bunk, really more of a cot, was along another gray wall. A stainless-steel commode/sink combo stuck out of the end wall, beneath the window. The third wall was the same gray color, but completely blank. The remaining equally gray wall contained only a very solid door, with a tiny glass window crisscrossed with wire mesh, inset at about eye level. The whole room was probably eight by ten feet. A cell, why call it anything else?

Later, another gendarme came in with a tray of food: a brownish meat dish that I didn't recognize, fake-looking whipped potatoes and Jell-O. Water to drink. It smelled okay, but I wasn't hungry. Nothing will kill your appetite like being imprisoned. I pushed the stuff around on the plate and ate some of the Jell-O. I set the water aside for later. I wasn't sure whether I would be able to bring myself to drink the tap water from the little sink, it being in such close proximity to the toilet. That insight was enough to tell me that I'd never survive in the Big House.

At what I guessed to be about six-thirty, Chief Malboeuf showed up. He had a different file with him, and was reading from it as he entered. Maybe it was the same file, but it had more paper in it.

"Monsieur McCann," he said, looking up at me. "May I call you Michael?" He pronounced my name with a funny French twist on it, but I didn't correct him. I considered it a good omen that we were potentially on a first-name basis.

"Sure," I said, standing up from where I had been sitting on the bunk, and offered my hand. He reached out uncomfortably and shook it weakly.

"I see here that you got a glimpse of the thief who stole your case," he said, pointing at the file.

"My case? Oh, my wallet, yes. I saw him briefly, as he turned away."

"Do you think you would recognize him if you were to see him again?"

I closed my eyes, trying to conjure up the image. The gypsy

kid popped up immediately from my memory. "I'm not sure, to be honest." I was not being at all honest. Never show all your cards.

He rubbed his chin as he stared at the open file. I sat back down on the bunk, leaving him standing in the middle of the small room.

"Don't you think that he was probably just one of the many run-of-the-mill Parisian pickpockets on the street, and that it was just a coincidence that my license got into the hands of someone who was in those offices?" I asked. "Maybe the attackers bought the stolen credit cards and my license from him."

"We've considered that," he replied, "and haven't ruled it out. But the two events were relatively close in time..." He let that thought float as he continued reading from the file. I let him read. Once again, I had nothing else to do.

"Michael," he said after about ten seconds, "we would like to enlist your help in this situation. We feel that the possibility that you may have actually seen someone involved in this... this group, might prove to be an advantage for us."

"I'm happy to help, but don't you think that would be a wild goose chase? Paris is a big place, what are the odds of me running into this guy?" I expected him to exhibit some inter-lingual confusion over the "wild goose chase" part, but he didn't.

He was clearly considering something else. "You are right, of course. But let me share some information with you."

"Go right ahead."

He paused, choosing his words carefully. "Although the general populace may be currently unaware," he said, "we are a city under siege. We have few leads on who these terrorists are, or where they might be planning to strike again. We are desperate for anything, even the smallest thing, that will help us gain a perspective on this situation."

My turn to consider. I had no idea how big of a deal this

had become, as I had been shut off from the rest of the world for most of the day. It must have been big, though, for someone in Malboef's position to present it to me that way. I immediately reached a decision. "As I said, I'm happy to help. But you've got to let me out of here and stop treating me like a suspect or a prisoner."

"Oh, of course," he said quickly. "And, as I said before, we apologize for the inconvenience. But to be honest, you remain a suspect of certain status, just based on the evidence."

I could live with that. "Just get me out of here," I said. "That's all I ask at this point."

"I will have a driver deliver you to wherever you choose. But keep in mind that I am expecting your assistance, so please remain available. And... I will be retaining your passport."

Not a surprise, really, but it was disappointing. My freedom would not be absolute.

Malboeuf walked me downstairs to an office where a female gendarme returned my stuff. He then delivered me to another suit seated at a desk in a nearby room filled with small cubicles. There was quite a bit of discussion in French, and Malboeuf didn't bother to interpret any of it for my benefit. The suit escorted me back to the parking garage, where we took a Mercedes mini-van out into the streets of Paris. This time I was allowed to ride in the front seat. Inwardly, I was feeling elated and liberated. I had been "detained" for less than six hours, but the feeling of relief at being released was delicious. I gave the driver Cherie's address, and he maneuvered the streets at a more sedate pace than had my previous driver. I took in the city views as we worked our way back to the 8th Arrondissement, almost feeling like a tourist again. Almost, but not quite. I wasn't sure at that point whether Paris would ever have that feel for me again.

I used my key to get into the house, calling out "hello" as I entered. There was no response. It appeared that everyone was out. I hoped I was still welcome. I went down into the basement, and found that my backpack was still there, open and in disarray on the bed. It had obviously been searched by the inspectors, but at least they hadn't pulled the contents out to fling them all over the room, the way an American cop might have done it. I did a quick check and found that everything appeared to be in place and intact, except for my passport, and I knew where that was. I took a shower until I had depleted the hot water supply, which wasn't very long, dried off with the towel hanging from a hook by the stall, and slipped into my boxers and T-shirt. I noticed that a couple envelopes had been placed on my pillow and, opening them, discovered that my replacement credit cards had arrived. Maybe I would need to use them to post bail.

I sat on the bed and realized, not to any surprise, that I was absolutely exhausted. I stretched out, and I was asleep before I could even adjust the pillow under my head.

TWENTY-TWO

I am standing on a beach along the Oregon coast, just north of Newport. The weather is glorious; cool, crisp, sunny and clear as a bell, a rare perfect late-September day. The wide, sandy beach is nearly empty, but for my family. I watch as my kids frolic in the cold Pacific surf. They are adorable in their tiny wetsuits, like little black seals, as they dive and splash in the greenish churning surf. Peter is twelve, Lauren ten and Richard seven. Patty sits further up on the sand, wrapped in a Navajo-print blanket, sunglasses atop her head, reading a book. She squints at the page as the wind whips her hair back and forth across her face. She ignores it, her attention fiercely on the page.

I turn around to view the sandy cliffs which rise up behind me to the grassy bluff above, where there are white and weathered cedar houses perched majestically above the beach. The views from those houses, I know from experience, are breathtaking. The sun is warm on my shoulders as I turn back to watch the kids. I look across the surf at the afternoon sky where it nearly touches the ocean's horizon. A thin marine layer of clouds is caught at the border between the two. I look at the kids. I look at my lovely wife. It is an idyllic scene.

I am happy, I think to myself. But I am lonely. How can that be possible in a life filled with so much activity, people and things? Barely a moment's rest from the seemingly endless soccer matches, school functions, family gatherings, work obligations. I am living the American dream; three beautiful kids, a wonderful spouse, a thriving professional practice. I have nothing to be unhappy about, and I'm not. But I am lonely.

I am, I realize, that way by nature. I tend not to create intimate friendships, or relationships that last for years and years. I have virtually no friends from high school, college or law school, no childhood friends that I maintain any sort of contact with.

I formulate no collegial relationships with my professional peers. I live half a continent away from my extended family and in-laws. I have a sister and a brother, neither of which I've had a conversation with in years. My parents are both deceased, and I have cousins, aunts and uncles whom I've never met. In this world of instant communication and global networking, I am almost completely isolated.

As far as the kids are concerned, I am involved and participatory, but I feel like an autopilot father. It definitely takes two full-time parents to get everyone where they need to be, on time, and with all the right stuff. Although I shoulder my portion of the responsibility, I feel like my efforts fall short of some undefined standard. I have done my share of homework assistance, bandaging scraped knees, breaking up fights and consoling broken hearts over the years, but I have never developed the kind of joined-at-the-heart type relationship that Patty has with the kids. She is such an amazing parent, and seems to come to the role so naturally. I don't think our children will ever, for one minute, think that their young lives were not filled with love and everything else they needed from their parents. I simply don't connect with them the way Patty does. It's not that I don't love the kids with all my heart, I do. I just don't have that all-encompassing connection and empathetic symbiosis that Patty has shared with each of them from the moment they were born. A natural, effortless thing that somehow evades me. I don't consider myself a bad parent at all, I just feel like I'm phoning it in much of the time.

The topic has come up a couple of times in my therapy sessions, but the therapist doesn't have any more insight into my feelings of isolation and loneliness than he does into my depression. It occurs to me that there might be some sort of connection between the two. He's not sure. Maybe I need a different therapist.

TWENTY-THREE

Deep in a dream, in some crazy imaginary landscape where everything defied logic, I had a warm sensation on the back of my neck. Gradually, I surfaced from the fog of sleep, oriented myself, and began to sort my way through to reality. The warm feeling was a soft breath on the bare gap between my hair and the collar of my T-shirt. I could smell soap, toothpaste and a delicious scent that I thought was lavender. If it wasn't, it should have been, it was what I had always imagined lavender smelled like. There was a warm, soothing sensation along my back, following the contours of my body. An arm was draped loosely over my side, a hand dangling lightly over my abdomen. The room was nearly black, with very little ambient light making its way into the subterranean space.

I rotated carefully onto my back, letting the arm stay in place. I turned my face toward the breath, and could feel the soft brush of hair against my cheek.

"I was trying not to wake you up." It was Cherie's voice, hushed and musical, inches from my ear. Being awakened in my bed by attractive women was something I could get used to.

"What time is it?" I asked.

"I have no idea. Late. Or perhaps early in the morning. Does it matter?" She shifted her weight and moved her hand up onto my chest, resting her head against my shoulder.

"I don't know if this is the right thing to say, but I'm glad you woke me up. I'm glad you're here."

She chuckled softly, throaty and enticing. "I'm glad you

woke up, too. To tell the truth, I couldn't have resisted the urge to wake you much longer."

I moved my hand to her forearm, stroking it lightly. "So, what are we doing here?"

"I guess that's up to you."

"Is Miranda upstairs?"

"She and Paul left in the afternoon, she needed to get back to school."

I took a deep breath, let it out slowly. "You know, I'm more than a little scared of your husband."

"Are you afraid of his... his size? Or because he's a policeman? Or of the fact that he's still my husband?"

I thought for a second, staring into the darkness. "I would say 'all of the above', I guess."

"Are you married still?"

"No, not for several years now."

"Nevertheless, you are a moralist, I think."

I cocked my head slightly. "I've never really heard it put that way, but yeah, I guess. More or less."

"I find that quite endearing," she said quietly. "Rare in a man these days."

She shifted her weight again, moving just a tiny bit closer. Her cheek pressed into my shoulder. "Just hold me," she said, her voice a soft whisper.

I rolled over to face her, sliding my arm under her neck, pulling her close. Our foreheads and the tips of our noses were touching, and I could make out the features of her face, even in the near absence of light. I ran my hand along her side, over her hip, down onto her bare leg. She was wearing, or not wearing, the same sleeping attire that she had worn the night before. My hand came to rest at the apex of her hip. We lay that way in silence for several minutes. I tried to turn slightly as I felt myself growing hard against the firmness of her thigh. Oh crap.

"Is this the American way, to be holding me down there,

below the sheets?" she said, a little breathlessly. Her eyes darted downward and her hand lightly touched the lower part of my abdomen.

"I have no control over that."

"Oh, I think you do."

I closed my eyes and smiled. I may have been a "moralist", but I wasn't dead.

TWENTY-FOUR

M orning arrived with pale light spilling down the stairway from the open door and the smell of coffee wafting from the kitchen. I rolled over and pulled the covers up against my chin, savoring the smell. It was mixed with the other smells from the bed, dominated by the one I was calling lavender. Reluctantly, I slid out of the bed, stood and stretched my arms up toward the ceiling, pushing my palms flat against the rough plaster. It was a low ceiling.

The stairs creaked in protest as I ascended them. I hesitated as I neared the top and heard low murmurs of conversation. We were not alone.

I stepped into the bright kitchen and saw Cherie directly in front of me, her back turned. She was standing at the sink, rinsing something under the tap. She had on a dark blue robe, tied with a cloth belt at the waist. Her hair was up, stacked on her head and held in place by a white elastic band.

I looked to my right and saw Gregor seated at the table, a steaming cup of coffee in front of him. "Good morning," he said, lifting his cup and taking a noisy slurp from it. I could only stare in reaction. Was there a change in his attitude? Did I detect sarcasm? Hard to tell.

Cherie turned quickly, smiling at me. "You slept like the dead," she said. "You must have been exhausted."

I glanced at the clock over the sink and saw that it was almost nine-thirty. "Yesterday was a very long day," I said. "Is there any more of that coffee?"

"Of course!" Cherie replied, no hint of stress in her voice.

I sat at the table opposite Gregor and tried to get a read on his mood. He had relapsed into his default mode, as inscrutable as ever. He sipped his coffee loudly and stared at the tabletop. I felt self-conscious sitting there in my boxers.

Cherie delivered my coffee with a bright smile. "Your mug, sir," she said, placing the same white ceramic mug that I had used the previous day in front of me, her hand on my shoulder. I lifted the mug and took a healthy swig. Fortunately, it wasn't scalding hot.

"Chief Malboeuf sent me to fetch you," Gregor said, looking up from his cup. "He has got me on temporary assignment from my department. Seems he carries much weight. I'd rather be doing my job than chauffeuring you around." There was the old familiar Gregor. Okay, at least I knew where things stood.

"Where are you taking me?" I asked. I did not relish the idea of spending another day in "detention".

"I don't know," he replied. "No one has shared that with me. I'm told only to collect you and bring you to his station. Seems there have been developments."

"Are you supposed to take me into custody?" I took another sizable hit of coffee.

"No, not my instructions. I'm told to bring you down to assist in the case. I'm to stay with you."

I wondered what "developments" had occurred and wondered anew how I was going to help, but I fully intended to keep my promise to Malboeuf. Anything to avoid further time in a cell. And he still had my passport. "Let me get dressed, then," I said, gulping down the remainder of my coffee.

"Here," Cherie said, motioning for me to give her the mug, "I'll make you another, you can take it with you."

Gregor remained silent as I left the kitchen for the basement. Cherie gave me a smile and a wink as I passed. It made me a little nervous. I think she was enjoying it.

Jeans, a light sweater, and Nikes; it seemed like a suitable outfit for assisting the Terrorism Brigade of the French National Police. Not really, but it was all I had. I shoved my hair into its normal haphazard array, stuffed my pockets with phone, credit cards and cash, and brushed my teeth at the little sink. I grabbed my jacket, but didn't put it on. The weather out the window had looked somewhere between fair and partly cloudy, so I figured I was covered.

Cherie met me at the top of the stairs with my coffee. "Be careful," she said quietly.

"I will try not to spill," I said, grinning.

"You know what I mean. Don't do anything idiotic. What would I do with your stuff if you didn't return?" She had probably gone through that mental exercise the day before, after the cops hauled me off. I touched her on the arm, smiled reassuringly and stepped into the entryway, where Gregor was waiting.

"Let's go, then," he said, opening the door and walking out. I balanced my coffee mug and followed, pulling the door closed behind me.

Gregor had cleaned out the passenger seat and floor for me. Or, I assumed it was for me. Maybe he'd had a date last night. I settled into the worn seat for the ride. The muffler still rattled and clanked, we didn't need the windshield wipers or the heat, and Gregor remained silent. I looked out the window and caught a glimpse of the Eiffel Tower in the distance. That was probably as close to tourism as I would get for the day. Gregor lit up a cigar, not bothering to crack his window, flicking his ashes on the floor of the car. I wasn't concerned about the possibility of fire, there wasn't much carpet left, at least where I could see. I was, however, concerned about suffocation, but I'd be damned if I was going to say anything. I tried to find pockets of clear air to breathe and pretended to look at the scenery.

We approached the iron gate at the old stone building, but it didn't open automatically as it had for the BMW. Gregor pulled up to a security box mounted next to the gate, rolled down his window and held his police ID up to a lens protruding from the front of the box. A green light on top of the box came on, a buzzer sounded, and the gate swung open. We drove down into the parking garage, and Gregor parked in a space at the far end marked *"Visiteur"*. I left my coffee cup in the car, assuming it would be returned to Cherie.

We took the elevator up to the squad room, where the same two original suits were waiting for us. It appeared that only their ties had changed. Older guy pointed at some chairs along the wall, and I sat obediently. A secretary offered me coffee in a Styrofoam cup, which I gladly accepted. Gregor wandered off, striking up a conversation with a guy at one of the desks. There was a lot of activity in the room, but all of the communication was in French, so I just watched the interaction, trying to get a read on what was happening. Without much success.

Malboeuf entered the room at a near run, cell phone to his ear, and everyone immediately turned their attention to him. He was fully suited up today, his jacket on and tie cinched tightly up to his collar. He rapid-fired some instructions, grabbed the younger suit's arm and motioned for me to follow. Gregor saw the exchange and fell into step behind me as I trailed Malboeuf into the hallway and onto the elevator. Malboeuf continued talking on the phone as we rode down to the garage, and finally clicked off as we approached what looked like the same black BMW that I had arrived in the day before. Younger suit got in behind the wheel, Malboeuf into the passenger seat, and Gregor and I piled into the back. We were underway before all the doors had slammed shut, the squeal of rubber on concrete echoing in the confined space. The gate was open before we hit the driveway, and the heavy sedan bottomed out as we slammed up the ramp and careened out onto the cobblestone street. Malboeuf said something to the driver, and he nodded, gunning the engine and weaving through traffic.

I wasn't familiar enough with Paris to know anything

other than that we were headed generally south and east. We moved from the narrow streets in the older part of town onto some wider boulevards, where we really picked up the pace. Evidently, the French national police don't use lights and siren when they are speeding through Paris. Or maybe we weren't equipped with them. Whichever it was, we flew through the congested streets silently.

There was a terse conversation going on between Malboeuf and the driver as we drove, and I saw Malboeuf point out the Autoroute entrance ramp, which we took. If I thought we'd been moving quickly along the boulevards, the A3 introduced us to a whole new level of speed, and it felt like we were pulling some G's as we entered the Autoroute. It was all I could do to keep my coffee from spilling.

Not long after we had merged into the six-lane trafficway, Malboeuf pulled a sheet of paper from a file he had in the front seat and passed it back to me. On it was a copy of a mug-shot photo of a very young man, a kid, middle-eastern in appearance, under bad lighting and in obvious distress. "Do you know him?" he asked.

I looked at the picture. "No, should I?"

"This is not your pickpocket?"

"Nope," I said, shaking my head, handing the picture back to him. He put it back in the file without further comment and got back on his phone.

I looked at Gregor, hoping that I might initiate some communication between us, quietly asking him: "What's going on?" while holding onto the armrest as we swerved between lanes.

"That young man in the photo turned himself in earlier," he said. "He admits to being one of the terrorists." Gregor paused, looking out the window nervously. "As to our current destination, there were some suspects spotted near Porte de Vincennes," he explained. "They were wearing the same tactical clothing that the attackers at the newspaper wore. One of the witnesses thought they saw guns. We are headed there now."

Malboeuf turned and looked at me. He had overheard Gregor's translation. He looked like he was going to add to it, but he didn't. He watched me for several more seconds, then turned back to watch the road.

I finished off the last of my coffee, setting the cup down on the floor. I rubbed my eyes with fingers still warm from contact with the cup. I wasn't thrilled about speeding into the heart of the action. It appeared that I had no choice in the matter.

TWENTY-FIVE

We exited the A3 at Porte de Vincennes, slowing down abruptly as we entered the streets of the Paris suburb. Malboeuf and the driver were looking for a specific address, Malboeuf using the map function on his phone, and the driver scanning streets signs and addresses as he drove. Gregor and I looked out the windows; he probably knew what we were looking for, I didn't. We pulled up in front of a small office building, where a uniformed gendarme officer was standing outside of his squad car talking to four women on the sidewalk. There was another police vehicle parked across the street, and several detective-types were milling about in front of the building. Gregor said something to Malboeuf as we pulled to the curb, and those two jumped out and headed directly toward one of the detectives, who waved at them in greeting. The driver and I stayed put.

I could see from a distance that the conversation was animated; much gesticulation, pointing and positioning for better views. It also seemed that Gregor knew the detective they were talking to, and he was being included in the conversation. All three of them walked over to the four women, who I took to be the witnesses, and spoke with them in some detail. More pointing and gesticulation, this time mostly by the witnesses. They finished and walked back toward the car, in no particular hurry.

"Longshot," Malboeuf said as he got in. "The witnesses are fairly uncertain about what they saw. Guys in black, basically."

"Well," Gregor said, planting his sizable mass onto the rear seat, "one of them described the tactical pants accurately. And she was reasonably sure that they had some sort of balaclavas or masks in their hands."

"Not much to go on," Malboeuf said dismissively. "In this weather, they might have been regular stocking caps."

"Where did they see them?" I asked.

"Over there," he said, pointing across the street in front of where the police car was parked. "But they got into a car and drove off."

"Unfortunately," Gregor added, "none of them know cars. Didn't know the make or model, not even sure of the color. Just 'darkish'."

"We'll make a couple circuits of the area," Malboeuf said. "They're probably long gone by now." He said something to the driver, and we pulled away from the curb. "Let's assume they are still in the vehicle."

We began winding through the narrow streets. It was a real change from our high-speed run on the Autoroute. I wasn't very invested in the search, I sided with Malboeuf, I felt like it was a waste of time. The driver, ever obedient, peered into every oncoming vehicle, down every side street and alley. Gregor was equally vigilant, probably just happy for something to do that resembled police work. I was leaned back in my seat, haphazardly casting glances at passing cars. I turned toward the side window, catching something remotely familiar out of the corner of my eye.

Son of a bitch. "Stop the car," I said emphatically. "Stop right now."

"What is it?" Malboeuf asked, turning around in his seat.

"In that car we just passed, a black Renault I think, I saw someone. The kid, I think. The kid that stole my wallet."

"Are you sure?"

I hesitated. "As sure as I can be. Under the circumstances."

Malboeuf barked an order, and the driver slammed on the brakes, squealed to a stop and executed a rapid K-turn in the narrow street. Evidently the BMW did have lights and siren, because they both came on as we sped back in the direction that the Renault had disappeared.

Within a couple of blocks, we caught up to the Renault. The car slowed and began to pull to the curb when three of the four doors suddenly flew open, spilling passengers out into the street and onto the sidewalk. The Renault then sped away, leaving a dingy cloud of smoke and three fleeing figures in its wake.

"*Merde*," I heard Malboeuf mutter as he opened his door, stepping into the street. He yelled something at the departing occupants of the Renault, and then shouted a short instruction back to the driver, who began moving forward as soon as Malboeuf had cleared the door. By this time Gregor was out of the car and pursuing the Renault passenger that had bailed out on his side. I quickly got the door open and stumbled out as the BMW sped away. I had no desire to be a passenger in a high-speed chase. I'd had enough race driving for the day, thank you.

I stood in the street for a second, and then fell into step behind Gregor. It seemed like the logical thing to do, since I now had no doubt that the fleeing figure which he was chasing was my pickpocket. There was something about seeing the kid in motion, even from the rear, which made me certain it was him. That certainty was reinforced when the guy turned and looked back over his shoulder to see if he was being pursued. Our eyes locked for a brief second, and then his gaze shifted to Gregor moving toward him, and they widened in alarm. He ducked his head and began running in earnest. Meanwhile, Malboeuf was pursuing the other two occupants, who were headed in the opposite direction. His gait was ungainly and he reminded me of a giraffe, all legs, neck and nose. I looked back for Gregor and saw him closing in on the pickpocket, running along the building opposite where the BMW was disappearing down the street.

Gregor could move well for a guy his size, and I had trouble keeping up with him. We saw the guy we were chasing duck around a corner and disappear, and Gregor got to the same corner at least ten yards ahead of me. I turned the corner just in time to see Gregor's large ass dart down an alleyway off the right side of the street.

All at once, several things happened; my legs decided that this running thing was not in their job description and they immediately went on strike; my lungs stopped taking in air, leaving me with the sensation that someone had thrown a plastic bag over my head; and, lastly, the side of the building on my right and the concrete sidewalk beneath me conspired to beat me about the head and face as they threw me into the gutter. Suddenly, I was on my back, gasping for air, seeing nothing but gray sky and vertical buildings. Had I tripped? I didn't think so. My head hurt. Had I passed out? I wasn't sure. I didn't remember things going black. I was a little dazed and confused. Was that phrase from a song or a book? Or maybe a film or television show? I fought the brain fog. I needed to move. Here we go, getting up and moving.

But I didn't move. My mind tried to do it, but my body refused. I tried to take an inventory of my arms, legs, fingers, toes, but there was no internal communication going on. I could hear wires fritzing and breakers tripping as circuits overloaded inside my head. A dark curtain started to close in from the edges of my vision, but I fought it off, blinking away the blackness. The cool air felt good on my face. I would just lay here and rest a bit.

In a few seconds, I looked up to see Gregor's face staring down at me. "I lost the little prick," he said. "Are you alright?" All I could do was raise my eyebrows in response. "You're not alright," he said emphatically. I agreed, but couldn't concur. He kneeled next to me; his big face closer. He pulled his phone out of his jacket pocket and spoke in French to someone on the other end.

I struggled to sit up, and Gregor helped me up onto the sidewalk as he talked on the phone tucked between his ear and shoulder. I found something sticky on the side of my face, and my fingers came away with blood on them. I traced the flow up the side of my forehead to a very sore swollen gash just along the hairline above my right temple. As I sat staring at the blood on my hand, Gregor produced a white handkerchief from his jacket and dropped it into my open palm. I did my best to dab and wipe away the blood, but it was difficult without being able to see what I was doing.

Gregor finished his conversation and stowed his phone away. "Can you walk?" he asked.

"I think so," I said, rising up on one knee. He steadied me as I stood cautiously. I brushed the dirt and street debris from my clothes and stretched a little as I regained my balance.

"What happened?" Gregor asked. "Here," he said abruptly before I could answer, taking the handkerchief from my hand and placing it against my head. "Hold this there."

I raised my hand and held the makeshift bandage in place. "I'm not sure what happened. I fell, obviously. One second I was running along behind you, the next I was on the ground."

Gregor supported me as we started walking back toward the spot where we had gotten out of the car. I was steadier with each step, and was quickly okay on my own. I continued to hold the handkerchief on my head as we emerged into the street where we had started our chase. A police vehicle suddenly came at us from the left, lights and siren, and another sped up from behind us with the same display. Then a black van came to a screeching halt to our right, and a squad of SWAT-type gendarmes jumped from the rear and side doors, hitting the ground at a dead run toward the direction that we had last seen Malboeuf pursuing the two other occupants of the Renault.

"What the hell?" Gregor said quietly, echoing my own thoughts. The officers from the two squad cars began setting up a perimeter, moving spectators and bystanders to the far side of the street. When they got to us, Gregor pulled out his police ID, talking to them in low tones as they looked at it. They waved us on, and Gregor led the way as we crossed the street and made our way toward the action, which appeared to be at the front of a grocery market just beyond a small park lined with flowers. As we crossed through the greenery on the far side of the park, we heard the distinct sound of gunshots up ahead. Gregor immediately dropped to the ground, pulling me down with him. We were on the dirt, among the flowers, behind a concrete barrier that closed off the far end of the park to traffic.

"Those were gunshots, right?" I asked. Gregor nodded his head. We both scrambled closer to the barrier, crouching behind it.

"We should stay here," he said, "until we know what is going on."

Another black van pulled up behind us, and another squad of combat-ready gendarmes ran past us, further down the street toward the market, trampling the flowers underfoot as they ran. We could see them deploy along both sides of the street, taking up tactical positions behind cover, staggered along the block.

I checked the blood flow from the gash on my head. It had slowed but not stopped. I refolded the handkerchief so that a clean section of white was exposed, and pushed it back against my head.

Meanwhile, Gregor was on his phone again. He kept his tone low, and his end of the conversation sparse, but the other party seemed to have a lot to say. Gregor ended the call and looked at me.

"It seems that this has turned into a hostage situation," he said. "The other two, the ones Malboeuf ran after, they are armed and have taken hostages inside that store." He motioned with his head toward the market on the other side of the barrier from us. "They are certain that at least one hostage has been shot."

"Shit," I said. Not eloquent, but it summed things up.

"I should not have you here," Gregor went on. "But I don't know how to get you to anywhere safer. And I was told to stay with you." He looked at me like I was a dog turd he couldn't get off of his shoe. I tried to look innocent, apologetic and not quite as terrified as I actually was.

Then, all at once, the world turned upside-down.

TWENTY-SIX

*T*he hospital waiting room is freezing, like a meat lock-
er. I cross my arms over my chest and lean down over
my legs, trying to capture some body heat. Although Legacy
Good Samaritan is a large, busy hospital, there are only two
of us waiting in the room. Mary, the older social worker
from the police station, is the other person. I have given her a
ride to the hospital from the station after she sent the younger worker home to be with her husband. I look around the
room, noting the absence of people.

"Does P have any family?" I ask her.

"Well, Dad's in jail. Mom has been AWOL on a drug bend-
er for several days. Typical."

"I know about them, but what about grandparents, extended family?"

"In the two years I been on this case, I haven't seen any-
body else."

I think back to the court proceedings and realize that she's
right. No one else had been present for any of them.

A young doctor in blue surgical scrubs enters the room.
"Perenzez Harris?" he says to the room, but he is looking at
us.

"Yes." I say.

He walks over, clearly trying to figure out our connection. I'm a white guy, old enough to be the child's grandfather, or even great-grandfather in P's world. Mary is African
American, not one of the ingredients present in P's racial
cocktail.

"Guardian Ad Litem, Social Worker," I say, pointing first to myself, then Mary.

"I see," the doctor says, taking a seat across from us. He has a dark beard shadow, his scrubs are creased and soiled, and his face shows a weariness that evidences the waning hours of a long shift. My guess is that he's a resident. He pushes the little surgical cap back on his head and leans forward. "I'm Dr. Colsen." He offers his hand to each of us, and we shake it, introducing ourselves.

"Perenzez has gone into surgery," he says. "I'm part of the trauma team that saw him when he was admitted. The surgeons will be doing several things to try to address his injuries, and it is hard to say how long he will be in there." He pauses and takes a breath. "He was in pretty bad shape when he came in. Given the status of his condition, they will probably not want to keep him under too long. But there's a lot to do."

"Should we wait?" I ask.

He thinks for a second. "Given the fact that you're here in professional capacities, I would say not. Is there no family?"

"Not that we know of," says Mary.

"If you'll leave me your contact information, I'll notify you when he's out of surgery," the doctor says. He pulls out his phone and takes down our numbers, entering them with a small stylus that he pulls from the body of the device.

We are riding in the elevator to the hospital parking garage when Mary sighs heavily and says: "Oh Lord, I'm not sure how much longer I can do this job. My heart breaks for those kiddos." She dabs at her eyes with a finger. She is wizened and battle-hardened, and probably not yet fifty years old.

The elevator doors open and we walk to my car. I push the button on my key fob, the car chirps and flashes, and we get in. It is nearly midnight.

Mary fastens her seatbelt over her considerable bulk, holds her purse on her lap, and sighs again. The tears glisten against the dark skin of her cheeks as I start the car.

TWENTY-SEVEN

The concussions from the explosions that emanated from the area of the market were as forceful as if the concrete barrier had been nonexistent. The rattle of gunfire that followed was disorienting, and I found myself moving closer to Gregor's bulk, clutching at the edges of the barrier.

"Flash-bang grenades," Gregor said. I wasn't sure if he was talking to me or himself. The sound of glass shattering, the broken pieces raining down on concrete, followed immediately, and smoke filled the narrow street in front of us. I could see the reflection of flames in the storefront window panes to either side of us, but I couldn't tell if it was muzzle flashes or something actually on fire. Pieces of wood, glass and other debris were flying past us and over us, beyond the barricade and out into the street. There were vivid flashes of something like strobes bouncing off of the building fronts. The smell of gunpowder and burning plastic was overpowering.

The barrage went on for what seemed like an eternity, but was in fact only a minute. As the chaos began to diminish, I saw Malboeuf round the corner of the nearest building at a full run, phone to his ear, looking as if he were loping across the Serengeti Plain. He turned suddenly upon seeing us and loped our direction, phone still in hand, dropping to a crouch next to Gregor.

"We have to go," he said emphatically. I could barely hear him, due to the ringing in my ears and the noises surrounding us.

"Where?" Gregor asked, looking around behind us.

"Back to the car," Malboeuf said, motioning toward the street with his phone.

I glanced in the direction he was waving and saw our black BMW pulling up to the curb. I was sure from the motion of the vehicle that there was a screeching of tires that accompanied the stop, but there was too much other noise to hear it.

Gregor grabbed the sleeve of my jacket, and before I even realized what was happening, we were sprinting toward the car. He pushed me into the rear door, and then followed behind me. By the time Malboeuf had reached his door, flung it open and piled himself in, we were already underway. The tires scrabbled for traction in the debris as we tore away from the curb.

"You are injured?" Malboeuf asked as he turned and saw me holding the blood-stained handkerchief to my head. I pulled it away and looked at it, realizing the blood on it was now dry.

"I'm fine," I said, touching the gashed area of my forehead. It was still sore, but no longer bleeding. I laid the soiled hand-kerchief on the seat beside me. Malboeuf nodded and turned back toward the streets.

"He fell," Gregor said, to no one in particular.

A short blast through the narrow lanes took us onto a wide but uncongested street, where we made good time, and we took a direct route to a marked access for the Autoroute.

We hit the on-ramp to the N2 Autoroute at what had to be more than seventy miles per hour. I was tempted to look over the driver's shoulder at the speedometer, but I knew that it would show only kilometers per hour, and I didn't know how to make the conversion accurately. Maybe it was best that I didn't know. Getting onto a major highway only increased our speed. The N2 is primarily a commercial route, so there were lots of trucks and other traffic to contend with, but our driver whipped by them like they were standing still.

As we cleared the Paris metro area, the traffic thinned, and we moved up to an even faster pace. Malboeuf and the driver exchanged a few words, and Malboeuf spent some time on his phone, making and receiving calls, but the interior of the car was mostly quiet. No one explained where we were going or why we were in such a hurry to get there. I was, clearly, just along for the ride. I settled back into the seat and hoped the driver was as good as he seemed to think he was. I looked over at Gregor, and he appeared to be deep in thought.

Before too long we started to slow, so I sat up and looked ahead. The road signs indicated several possible options, and we exited to take a road toward Dammartin-en-Goële, which I took to be our destination. We hugged the curves of what I would refer to as a "county road", a two-lane highway, at a reduced rate of speed, but we were still moving right along. Gregor, too, became more interested, leaning over to see past Malboeuf's head.

We rounded a curve and were suddenly in the midst of what looked like a reenactment of the Normandy invasion. Or the siege of Leningrad. Or Woodstock. There were police cars and trucks, Fire Brigade units, ambulances, armored assault vehicles and assorted emergency traffic as far as the eye could see. Most of them had their blue-and-red lights flashing, and it produced an eerie effect in the hazy midday light. There were uniformed gendarmes, militarily-clad and traditional, as well as a lot of suits and ties running around, some with guns. We pulled up to a checkpoint, and Malboeuf rolled down his window, speaking briefly to the guy manning the post. We proceeded on, winding our way through all the parked vehicles, toward the center of the action.

We hadn't made it all the way to Dammartin-en-Goële, but I could see the village in the distance. We were in a rural area, just beyond the outskirts of the little town. The epicenter of the event seemed to be a crossroads, with two small farmhouses in the southeast quadrant of the intersection. Both were small, white stucco-sided bungalows with slate roofs, probably several hundred years old, and one had a sagging wood-on-stone porch with sections of the wrought-iron railing missing in several places. Opposite the farmhouses, in the northwest quadrant, was a large metal industrial building which looked completely out of place in the otherwise bucolic setting.

We left the road and drove across a field toward the metal building. There was a cluster of men and vehicles in the parking lot and driveway blocking our access, so we parked on the grass in the field adjacent to the paved area. The gray front of the building was separated from the parking lot by a pipe railing, about three feet high and painted white, that looked like it was designed to demark the edge of the parking area and prevent vehicles from driving into the side of building. We sat in the car for several minutes, and then an older guy in a suit emerged from the building and motioned toward us. Malboeuf got out, conversing with him from a distance over the open door. He leaned back into the car.

"Michael," he said, "please come with me."

I got out and walked around the front of the car to follow him. Gregor and the driver stayed put. It was chilly and windy out in the open, and I was glad I'd grabbed my jacket. The ground beneath the brittle grass was slightly soft from the recent rain, and our feet sank in as we walked across it. There were places where the field had been torn up by all the activity, leaving everything from shoe-sized divots to large tire ruts. We wound our way through the crowd toward the building, eventually reaching the spot where the older guy was waiting. He turned and led us toward the front of the building. There was a constant stream of people moving past us, in and out of the entrance. The front door stood open, and there were muddy tracks running across the sidewalk, over the threshold and onto the concrete floors inside.

"*Vous pouvez entrer,*" the older guy said, motioning toward the doorway. Malboeuf walked past him, through the door, and I followed into the front room, which appeared to be the lobby of a business.

The room was a mess. The office furniture had been tossed around like it had been through a tornado, there was broken glass all over the floors, and the interior walls were torn to bits by bullet holes. Wooden splinters protruded from the window frames and some of the furniture. I could see daylight showing through holes in the metal exterior walls from the outside.

In the center of the room, laid out on a faded red Persian carpet, were the bodies of two men. They had obviously been placed there; they were too neatly aligned side-by-side to have fallen there naturally. The carpet was stained darkly in several places around the bodies. I could see multiple bullet wounds, and their clothing was soaked with blood. One of them had a head wound, and half of his face was a bloody mess. Both were a ghastly gray color, their eyes staring vacantly at the ceiling.

"Do you recognize either of them?" Malboeuf asked me. The question startled me, and I looked at him. He pointed toward the bodies. "Do you?"

I looked back at the two men, boys really. Both in their mid-twenties, dark-skinned, with black hair, slight-to-medium builds. They actually had a similarity beyond those basic characteristics, as if they might be related, but it was difficult to tell with the one's face being so messed up. Neither was at all familiar to me. Certainly, neither of them was my pickpocket. Gregor and I had chased him down an alley back in Paris. I had no doubt about that.

"No," I answered gruffly. Then I hurried out of the front door and threw up over the white railing onto the parking lot in front of the building.

TWENTY-EIGHT

*M*y therapist's name is Bob. Not Robert, or Rob or Dr. Patterson. Just Bob. When I first started seeing him it seemed very unprofessional to me. Now it seems to fit.

We have been discussing various matters, but I am avoiding the elephant in the room. He knows that I have recently had a very difficult conversation with my children, but he doesn't force the topic. I finally bring it up.

"So how did it go?" he asks me.

"As well as can be expected, I guess," I reply. "It's tough. The kids are pretty much grown, but they're still my kids. They love their mom."

"And they love you."

"Yeah."

"How do you feel about being the one who had to have that discussion with them?"

"I don't know. A little resentful, I guess. Like I had to clean up the mess."

Bob's response is silence. Bob is good at silence. I have come to understand that it means I should continue.

"That's really about it. Resentful."

"How are you doing with all this?"

I sigh. I know the answer, I'm just buying time. "Pretty shitty, really."

"Not surprising. Nothing wrong with that."

"I'm working on moving on."

"That's important, too. But there's no need to rush it. Move at your own pace."

"I know. I am."

Bob shuffles his papers and looks at the clock. Our time is just about up.

"I want you to work on something for next week," he says. "I want you to bring me a list of the top five things you want to happen next in your life. Can you do that?"

"Sure," I say, nodding.

"How are you feeling on the prescription I gave you?"

"Okay, I guess. It seems to be helping. I think. I don't really know, to tell you the truth."

"The truth, that's always good. Alright, we'll stick with it, see how it goes. You can refill it when you need to."

"Thanks."

I leave Bob's office and walk out into the bright sunshine of a clear October day, a relative rarity in Portland. The air has a slight chill to it at this point, a hint of the colder weather to come. I close my eyes and let the sun warm my face. It feels good.

TWENTY-NINE

Malboeuf had me by the elbow, leading me back toward the car. I paused to clear my throat and spit onto the grass.

"Are you alright?" he asked.

"I guess," I responded. "This isn't exactly everyday stuff for me."

"For me either," he said, guiding me onward. "At least not most days."

Gregor and the driver were standing outside the car as we approached. All four of us got into the car, and the driver made his way through the tangle of vehicles and personnel. No one said a word.

The trip back to Paris was more sedate, or at least a bit slower, than our previous sojourns. Fifteen minutes into the drive, I couldn't contain myself any longer.

"Chief Malboeuf," I said, as politely as I could, "I think I could use just a little information here."

"Such as what?"

"I don't know, such as who were those two dead guys you had me look at, and what was it supposed to accomplish?" I was attempting, without much success, to keep the sarcastic tone out of my voice.

Malboeuf turned in his seat to look at me. "I suppose I understand your frustration, but we are all frustrated right now." He reached across and rested his arm on the back of the driver's seat, behind the headrest. His slender fingers drummed softly on the black leather. "Those two men were brothers. They were involved in the attack on the newspaper staff. They robbed a store up here, and then we tracked them down to the location we just came from. They claimed that they wanted to die as martyrs." He paused, turning to look out the windshield. "They seem to have gotten their wish." He stared at the road for several seconds. "The other individual, the one I showed you the photo of, was also involved in the attack. He is currently in custody. The situation back in Porte de Vincennes has now been resolved. The hostages were freed and the gunman killed." I noted to myself that he had said "gunman", singular. My recollection was that he had taken off in pursuit of two people from the car, at least initially.

I pondered the information he had given me. "Alright, then. What about bringing me here? What purpose did that serve? Those two back there were already dead."

"As I told you before," Malboeuf said, "we are desperate for information, for connections. Your driving license is one of the few connections we have right now. Since you think that one of the men in the car was the one that robbed you, we can now follow up on that." He paused again. "And at the time we started out for this last location, the two brothers had not yet been killed. The challenging part of this kind of investigation is that you never know which little thing will open up a break." He looked thoughtful. "Michael, I don't know how to make you understand this, but there are many people dying in Paris. Too many of them. And it's on my watch."

There wasn't much more I could say, the guy was just doing his job. And, as far as I could tell, he seemed to be pretty good at it.

I had noticed, out of the corner of my eye, that Gregor had been fidgeting nervously throughout much of the conversation. I didn't know what that was about, but I intended to find out.

Malboeuf directed the driver to stop at a rest area with a convenience store. We all were feeling the effects of our morning coffee, and the car needed gas.

I found a restroom, used it, and got myself a bottle of water.

I walked out to the area in front of the store, where there were outdoor tables; ugly red metal things with attached benches, bolted down to the concrete, not exactly a Parisian sidewalk café setting. I could see the driver at the gas pump, filling the car. Malboeuf had disappeared.

I spotted Gregor smoking a cigar at the far corner of the building, got up and walk over to him. He nodded at me in a silent greeting.

"Gregor," I said, in as friendly a tone as I could muster, "I saw you react to Malboeuf's official line on my involvement in this thing. I take it you aren't completely on board with that."

Gregor drew on his cigar, letting the smoke encircle his face. He exhaled and looked at me. "Look, I don't know what I should or shouldn't be saying to you, but these are not my bosses." He hesitated slightly, then continued, scanning the parking lot and front of the store as he spoke. "It's plain as day, Malboeuf still has some suspicion of your involvement. He was looking for a reaction from you, or from those ter-rorists, if they'd been alive to give one. They have also been monitoring your credit cards. There has been quite a bit of activity on them, even though it appears that you notified the credit companies of the theft right away. I'm not sure how that aspect plays out in their view."

I thought about that, sipping on my water. "How about you? Are you in agreement with him?"

"As a policeman," he went on, "I have learned to trust my gut. My gut tells me you had no involvement in this." He stubbed out the cigar against the cinderblock of the building, checking the burned end for any lingering embers. He put the remaining length of cigar into the inner pocket of his jacket.

"Can't you tell them? I mean, how do I get Malboeuf off my back?"

"Oh, I have given them my input, but I'm afraid my gut isn't very high on Chief Malboeuf's list of reliable sources." He stood away from the wall and started walking toward the car.

I walked with him. "I realize that you haven't seen the media coverage, but this is a big fucking deal," he said.

"Yeah, I've figured that out," I said. "How many people died?"

"I believe the count is at thirteen victims," he said grimly. "Ten at the newspaper, and three police. I have heard that there are two more policemen in hospital, don't know the outcome there yet. All of the information is very sketchy at this point. And of course, there are the dead terrorists."

"Jesus," I said breathlessly, struggling to keep up with his long strides.

"It's been bloody," he said. "And no one knows how long it will go on. The whole city is in panic. There have also been demonstrations in public support of the victims, but those just look like more carnage waiting to happen. If I'm a terrorist, I'm salivating over those crowds gathering."

We reached the car, and I realized that the conversation had been the most I'd heard out of Gregor since we met. Maybe he was warming up to me. Or maybe I'd just gotten him on a topic he was passionate about: police work. The driver was standing near the front fender, scanning the parking lot and building, looking around for Malboeuf. Gregor and I both got in the car to wait. Malboeuf came around the corner of the store, still on his phone. He approached the car, said something to the driver, and got in. The driver started the car, ascended back onto the Autoroute and, although he restrained from breaking any more land speed records, he continued to drive at a pace far above the speed limit.

I retreated into a place inside my head, remembering the walls, windows and furniture at the industrial building, pocked with bullet holes. Lots of them. I could still hear the bombs and guns booming around me back at the market, the smell and feel of explosive gasses in the air. I slid down in the leather seat, wedging my knees against the back of the driver's seat to stabilize myself. The scenery outside whizzed by the windows in a nearly imperceptible blur.

THIRTY

I dozed a little in the car, even with our NASCAR-esque driver at the wheel. We arrived back at the Terrorism Brigade's offices late in the afternoon. Looking around the group as we rode the elevator, I could see that I was not the only one for whom it had been a long day.

Gregor was clearly exhausted, looking even more disheveled and older than usual. He had several layers of bags under his eyes, and his hair looked like someone had styled it with a hand-held mixer. His clothes, although rumpled and mismatched to begin with, now looked like they had been pulled out of a dumpster; there was a rip in the shoulder seam of his jacket, the knees of his pants were soiled and his shirt was stained with concentric rings of perspiration that had soaked it at various times during the day.

Malboeuf was more intact, but the dark circles under his eyes had reached zombie-like proportions, and his white shirt was badly in need of laundering and pressing. His collar was still buttoned to the top, but the tie hung down about an inch, and was skewed off to one side. His dark suit still looked fresh, and his shoes were still mostly shined, even though there were traces of mud along the sides and the soles.

I knew I looked like hell, even without a mirror. I could feel the crusted blood on the side of my face, and in my hair, and I could see that my jeans looked like I had been crawling through the gutter. Oh wait, I had been. The sleeve of my jacket was stiff from dried something-or-other, and I could detect a foul odor that I recognized as my own funk. I also noticed that Gregor and Malboeuf kept looking at me with concerned expressions, and then at each other with confirming glances. Maybe I really didn't want to see myself in a mirror.

Our driver was still relatively fresh in appearance. In fact, he looked to be fairly unaffected by the day, other than showing a little fatigue in his face and posture. Then again, he was decades younger than the rest of us, and he'd been safely ensconced in the car most of the day.

When we reached the squad room, Malboeuf sent me off with the driver to a small office where I could see medical supplies and equipment on the shelves. After a few minutes, a guy whom I took to be a doctor or medic came in, looked me over, and then roughly cleaned my head wound. Whatever he was using stung like hell, and I noticed that he didn't clean anywhere but the actual injury site, leaving the dried blood elsewhere intact. He taped a gauze bandage over the gash and indicated to the driver that I was good to go. We went back to the squad room, where I was directed to a chair, and I sat.

The room was a mass of action, with suited agents running all over the place, talking on phones, looking at maps, giving and following orders. Secretaries pulled fax sheets from machines, relayed phone messages and took notes. I noticed that it was a gender-specific staff, with the agents all being men, and the secretaries all being women. I slipped into sort of a numbed consciousness and just let all the activity play out around me. I realized at one point that I hadn't seen Gregor in quite a while, and wondered if he had gone off duty and had been relieved of me. Eventually, however, he wandered into the room and took a seat next to me. Back to form, he didn't say a word.

Just as I was sure I was going to nod off again, Malboeuf showed up, had a brief conversation with Gregor, and left hurriedly. Gregor turned to me and informed me that he was to take me home, as soon as we were contacted by someone named "Bref".

A few minutes later, a young black guy walked up and spoke to Gregor. He then extended his hand to me, saying: "*Bonne soiree,* Monsieur McCann. I am Agent Bref. I will be accompanying you." He looked like most of the other agents, except, of course, he was black. I hadn't realized until I saw him how homogenously white the Terrorism Brigade seemed to be. Let's see, I had now observed that they were potentially misogynistic and racist. An American lawyer could have a heyday here. Except that, as I had been so pointedly reminded of earlier, our Constitution didn't apply in this country.

Bref also broke the mold in the attire protocol. He had the standard-issue suit, but instead of the usual dress shirt and tie, he wore an ivory-hued turtleneck. He made it work, but it didn't give any of the hierarchical clues that I had picked up on earlier, due to the fact that he had no tie to fall into the subdued or flashy categories. His afro didn't fit with the agency-conforming haircuts, and it was somewhere between short and cropped, so I was at a complete loss as to where he fell on the inter-office power scale.

I shook his hand. "Nice to meet you Agent Bref, especially if meeting you means I'm about to get out of here."

Bref smiled, flashing dazzling white teeth, and then morphed his face into a wounded look. "Oh, I am sorry that you are so eager to depart our company." The smile returned. "But I fully understand your desire to leave. Yes, we will be taking you home."

The three of us walked to the elevator and rode down to the parking garage.

"We can take your car, Detective Wolfert," Bref said authoritatively. "You can run me back when we're done."

Gregor gave him a withering look, but didn't protest. When we reached the car, Bref opened the back door and some trash fell out onto the concrete. He stooped to retrieve it, and Gregor said, with some exasperation: "Leave it. It's all rubbish."

"Fine," Bref replied pleasantly, "Your call, then."

I noticed as Bref twisted his way into the rear seat of the car that he was wearing a gun in a shoulder holster under his suit coat, something I had become used to *not* seeing among the Terrorism Brigade guys. I had no idea what the official policy was, but clearly Bref was a little different from the other agents I had been exposed to.

Gregor drove in his usual careless way, and the muffler collided with the pavement even more frequently with the weight of a passenger in the rear seat. Bref didn't seem to mind the noise or the trash, and engaged me in conversation for most of the trip. By the time we reached Cherie's house, I was confident that I had been involved in an interview. Not really an interrogation, but there was some sort of agenda involved.

Cherie greeted us at the door, and immediately expressed concern over my head wound, leading me to the kitchen table and insisting on removing the gauze bandage to inspect it.

"It will only take a second, and I am a nurse," she said as she pushed me into a chair and removed the tape. Bref and Gregor looked on, seemingly unwilling to argue with her. She leaned over and inspected my head, prodding and squeezing lightly. She smelled great. She made a disapproving noise and said: "This should have been sutured. It will get infected or leave a scar. Who tended to him?"

Bref and Gregor both answered in French, and both sounded apologetic.

"Police medics, ha!" she responded. She laid her hand lightly on my shoulder. "Sit still, I will get some bandages and *antibiotique crème*." She was shaking her head as she pushed past the two cops and left the room.

Bref took a seat across the table from me. "I have been assigned to be your liaison," he said, "so that Detective Wolfert can return to his usual duties. I will be in touch after I return to the Brigade, but please let me know if you leave here." He took a card from the inside pocket of his jacket and placed it on the table in front of me. "You have a cell phone, I trust?"

"I do," I said. "My number is..."

"No need," he interrupted, "I can get it from Chief Malboeuf."

"I'm sorry," I said, "but I don't understand why I need a 'liaison'. I'm not going anywhere. Malboeuf has my passport."

"We still do not know where your connection to these events will lead," he said. "We feel that it is best that we remain in close contact with you as this dynamic situation unfolds."

"*Dynamic situation unfolds...*" I thought to myself. This guy was no regular street cop. No wonder Gregor had been so deferential. That, and Bref had a gun.

"Whatever," I said, waving my hand dismissively. I realized that I sounded annoyingly like my daughter Lauren when she had been about seventeen, but I couldn't help it, I was feeling very put-upon.

"Very well, then," Bref said, reaching to shake my hand as he stood. "I will be in touch." He said something in French to Gregor that sounded more like an order than a request just as Cherie came back into the room. "Thank you for your assistance," he said to her as she passed. She responded briefly in French, and it didn't sound very friendly. If anyone in the group thought it bizarre that I was being remanded into the care and comfort of Gregor's wife, no one expressed it. Bref and Gregor departed without further interaction as Cherie tended to my head.

"How did this happen?" she asked. Her manner had completely transformed into caring and soothing in the blink of an eye.

"I fell," I said, echoing Gregor's earlier description. She stopped applying the ointment and gave me a look which clearly indicated that my answer was insufficient. "We were running after a guy," I elaborated. "*The* guy, actually, the one who stole my wallet. I must have tripped on the cobblestones."

"You found him, then?" She sounded surprised.

"Not exactly 'found him'. More like stumbled upon him."

"And what did he have to say for himself?"

"Well, nothing. He got away. I fell, and Gregor lost him."

"Oh God, you two were playing cops and robbers! You and that stupid German policeman." She shook her head in annoyance.

"No, it wasn't really like that. Well, I guess it was, sort of. Gregor was doing his job. I probably should have stayed out of it."

She finished putting ointment and a few butterfly bandages onto my forehead, and stepped back to review her work. "It will do for now," she said, pushing my head to one side so that the light hit the area better, "but we really should have a doctor look at it. I still think it should be sutured." She covered the wound site with a fresh gauze bandage and affixed it with a couple pieces of white tape. The process was a little rough and I realized with some amusement that she was irritated with me.

"Right now," I said wearily, "what I need more than anything is some rest. I need to crawl into that bed downstairs and sleep for about a week. I hope you don't mind, but I don't think I can put it off for one more minute."

"I understand," she said, helping me up out of the chair. "Your bed is ready; the linens are cleaned." Her hand lingered on my shoulder for a moment. "Go, rest." She gave me a playful little push in the direction of the downstairs doorway. I didn't need to be told twice.

I took the stairs carefully, still feeling unsteady on my feet. I stripped off most of my clothes, rolled under the covers and was immediately unconscious.

THIRTY-ONE

I am looking across the expanse of cream-colored sheets that cover a king-size bed at the woman sleeping on the other side. Patty and I have been married for about two years, and we are as happy as can be. There are exciting events and plans for the future: her promotion to Vice President for Personnel at the bank where she has worked for three years; my decision to leave my family's practice and begin a legal career of my own with three other young, ambitious attorneys.

Then there is the matter of starting a family. We have discussed having kids as soon as she has the new job under control, and I have the new practice up and running. But we both acknowledge that there is never a "right" time to start a family, and that if you wait too long for it you may end up missing the boat altogether. We already have friends who have decided to wait to have kids until some specific align-ment of the stars, only to have difficulty conceiving, or just never reaching that ever-elusive sweet spot. We both know that it can become a matter of now or never, but we're not there yet.

I roll over onto my side and watch as the sheets rise and fall with Patty's breathing, the faint moonlight creeping over the bed from a small gap between the curtains on the win-dow above the headboard. I am thankful to her for bringing us to this place, and such is definitely the case. Her determi-nation to have a certain life, to achieve a very specific version of the American Dream, has brought us here. On my own, I might have meandered along, smelling the roses. Patty has kept both of us, or more specifically me, on a track defined by certain goals and parameters, on our way to arrive at a place of comfort and security. And children are a part of that. Two-point-five, I believe, is the average, although I'm unsure how that "point-five" part works. As I stare at Patty, the moon is covered by clouds and the muted light recedes from the bed, out the window, and into the night. I look at the space where her slumbering form has been enveloped by darkness, but can no longer make it out.

I roll back over to face the wall and wonder about where life will take us. I have reservations about the reliability of one of my partners, and I wish my father and brother were more supportive of me leaving their firm. Money is certainly tight, but we're young and that's to be expected. I guess I'll just keep plugging away and leave the strategic planning to Patty. It's her forte.

I close my eyes, and can tell very little difference from when they were open.

THIRTY-TWO

"This American could be a problem." The man with the missing finger was speaking to another man, one who had not been present during the events of the previous days.

The other man exhaled and gritted his teeth, but did not respond. He was older than the others, short and stocky with a balding, shaved head. His complexion was dark, but something made his appearance different from the rest, perhaps indicating another nationality.

"Dimitri says that he recognized him," the man with the missing finger went on, motioning toward the young man standing in the corner of the room. The young man looked fearful, but nodded slightly.

The other man still did not speak, only raised his eyes and squinted as he looked at the larger man before him.

The man with the missing finger held his gaze for several seconds before speaking.

"Just take care of it," he said firmly before turning abruptly and walking out of the room.

THIRTY-THREE

A dark, quiet basement and a soft bed make for good sleep. I floated my way up into reality, letting my senses wake up on their own terms. The first one that came to life was pain. My head hurt. Not just where I had the gash and bump on my noggin, but deep down in the neural synapses of my brain.

As the rest of me awakened, I began to formulate a fixation on getting some pain medication on board. I would have chewed a dozen aspirin without water if someone had offered them to me. As things were, however, that wasn't going to happen. I would need to get out of bed, on my feet, up the stairs and into the kitchen to score some relief.

I pulled on my jeans and a T-shirt and made my way up the stairs. I pushed the door open to find Cherie sitting at the table reading the paper.

"Good morning, Sleepyhead," she said cheerfully.

"Headache," was all I could say, grimacing as I did so.

"But of course," she said, quickly rising. "Here, sit."

I did so as she rummaged through a cabinet in the corner of the kitchen. "I have extra strength acetaminophen," she said. "But first, I need to know, are you dizzy or nauseous?"

"No," I said, trying not to move my head or speak too loudly. "Just in pain."

I watched as she shook several white caplets from the plastic container into her palm, then opened the refrigerator and removed the orange juice bottle. It was all I could do not to crawl on my hands and knees across the kitchen floor and wrest those pills from her grip as she calmly took out a glass and poured in some juice. She finally crossed the room and plopped the glass in front of me, offering up the acetaminophen. I scooped up the pills, popped them in my mouth, and slugged down several big gulps of juice. The physical relief would take a while, but the psychological surge of pleasure was immediate. I sighed and put the empty glass on the table.

"Goodness," she said, stroking my hair. "You must really be hurting."

"Mm-hmm," I said, "but not for long."

"Let me take a look at this," she said as her hand moved to my forehead, deftly pulling the bandage loose with a minimum of discomfort before I could even react. She gently grasped my jaw in her other hand and moved my head from side to side to view the wound site. Very different from the previous evening, when I'd felt like a dog being examined at the Westminster Kennel Club Show. I was beginning to get a sense of her moods, discovering that they could be mercurial; terse and rough one minute, gentle and soothing the next. But rather than finding it perplexing or annoying, I found it intriguing.

"It may look a little better, but I'm not sure." She rubbed the stubble on my jaw back and forth with her thumb.

"Sorry," I said, "I haven't had much of a chance to shave lately."

"Ah, I love your stubble! Very *robuste*. And *très* sexy." Her eyes sparkled as she grinned at me. This woman was intoxicating. "Maybe you should grow the beard. The mustache suits you. Dashing."

"I've had the mustache for years, since I was in my twenties," I said, "but it wasn't gray back then."

"It's very distinguished," she said, stroking the right side of my mustache with her index finger. "Very appealing." Her hand lingered on my upper lip, and she gazed into my eyes. Suddenly, she smiled. "Look at you," she said, "I think you are blushing!" She moved her hand gently on my stubbled cheek. "How sweet."

I cleared my throat. "I think the drugs are working. My headache is subsiding. A little." It was all I could come up with.

"I still think you should see a doctor."

"Let's see how things go today, okay?"

She touched my forehead lightly. She tried to make it affectionate, and it almost was, but I sensed that she was really checking to see if I had a fever. "All right," she said. "So, what shall we do today?"

"I'm not sure Agent Bref would approve of me going anywhere."

"Oh, surely he couldn't object to you walking to the market with me. That's on my list."

I thought about that. I resented even having to consider it. "Okay," I said, "just let me get a quick shower."

"Excellent!" she said, the megawatt grin on her face. "Go ahead and wash your cut, but gently. I'll reapply the gauze after."

I showered until, once again, the hot water ran out, then stooped over in front of the small mirror and considered shaving. The guy looking back at me had seen better days. He wasn't bad-looking to begin with, despite the ugly gash on his forehead, but he showed a lot of mileage. The permanently disheveled hair was gray-going-to-white, with a wiry mind of its own, and the lines around the eyes and mouth had become deep and embedded. The once-piercing blue eyes gazing out from beneath slightly shaggy eyebrows looked clouded and weary, but still had a spark of light smoldering in them.

I rubbed my hand over the gray stubble, recalling Cherie's words: "*très* sexy." She might have been teasing me, but what the hell. I toweled my hair dry and left the stubble.

I held up the jeans that I had been wearing the day before for inspection under the light, and realized that they needed to go into the laundry pile; there was filth from the gutter, mud from the scene at Dammartin-en-Goële, and dried blood from my head. I dug a fresh pair out of my backpack and tried to shake out the wrinkles.

My jacket was similarly soiled, so I opted for a sweatshirt over my T-shirt and hoped for some warmth in the air. The sun was shining, so there was at least some basis for optimism. My running shoes were muddy, but they were all I had. I knocked off as much of the dried mud as I could into the sink and washed it down the drain.

I glanced into the mirror again, checking the cut on my forehead. The gash was still red and angry-looking, and the corresponding bump was turning a gnarly shade of purplish-green. I had tried to go gently on the area during my shower, but a couple of the butterfly strips were coming loose. No problem, I had my own private nurse.

I reported for duty upstairs, let Cherie tend to my head wound, and we were off. She threw an anorak over her workout clothes and slung a large canvas shopping bag over her shoulder. We headed in the opposite direction of where I'd been previously, strolling along the sidewalk in front of the row houses that occupied the block. The narrow sidewalk forced us to walk close together, and before I knew it, Cherie had slipped her hand into mine. Not that I was complaining one bit. We walked like that, hand-in-hand, enjoying the bright sunshine and crisp morning air, for several blocks. Several times we encountered other walkers, and we moved aside to let them pass. We were in no hurry, and had all day to enjoy our excursion.

This neighborhood was very different from the Montmartre area, but equally as scenic in its classic French feel. Cherie pointed out, at one particular spot between buildings, where the Eiffel Tower was visible in the distance. I could also see the Basilique du Sacré Coeur above and behind us, on its hilltop perch. I was thinking to myself that it didn't get much better than this.

The walk, however, was mostly uphill, and I found myself struggling to get enough air into my lungs. I tried to cover it up, and Cherie didn't say anything, but not long after I started laboring, she patted my arm and said: "Almost there, just ahead."

We turned the corner and transitioned from a calm residential silence to an active commercial buzz. There were open-front markets and free-standing vendors lining both sides of the street, interspersed with store-front shops displaying wares in their large glass windows ranging from perfume to cheese. The smells that drifted forth from the various cafes and food vendors were tantalizing, and the kaleidoscope of color and texture on display, along the produce and flower bins, was nearly overwhelming.

"My favorite street in all of Paris," Cherie said, squeezing my hand. I'm sure she could tell from my smile that I shared her delight.

"It's unbelievable," I said. "I thought this kind of scene only existed in movies, a creation of Hollywood."

"And where do you think Hollywood got their inspiration?" she asked.

"And they really don't do it justice," I replied. "Especially not in the aroma department."

Cherie laughed. She pulled me by the arm toward one of the markets with a mixture of fruits, flowers, spices and vegetables on display out front. "There are a few things I need in here," she said.

We moved past the produce bins and into the tiny interior of the store. The proprietor waved to Cherie as we passed.

Inside the market, the floors creaked with antiquity, and the ancient shelves crowded the narrow aisles. The foodstuffs lining the shelves were both familiar and alien. Nabisco products were featured prominently, with French language labels. Packaging, overall, was much smaller than us Americans are accustomed to; very few "super-sized" or "family pack" portions available. Breakfast cereals seemed to be international; Wheaties, Froot Loops, Cheerios, all in evidence. I especially got a kick out of *"des céréales Croquet Cap'n"* (Cap'n Crunch).

Cherie had a small armful of items at the counter, where she and the store clerk chatted away as he rang her up. I noticed that one of the items was a twelve-pack of Starbucks K-cups. That made me smile even more.

With her purchases bagged, we headed back into the street, where Cherie picked up a long loaf of bread from a rack in the doorway of a bakery. The smells coming from inside were incredible. At that point I offered to carry the bag, and felt like a genuine Frenchman with my bread pointing upward out of the bag behind my shoulder. All I needed was a beret.

Cherie added a bunch of fresh flowers to my bag, and we spent twenty minutes sorting through produce from a candy-striped display cart in the warming sun. A selection of apples, pears and a couple of peppers made the cut, and went into the bag.

We sat under the yellow canopy of a bistro and enjoyed espressos as we watched the bustling marketplace.

"This is beautiful," I said to her between sips of espresso, "exactly how I have always pictured Paris. Is this anything like the famous Rue Cler? I read that it is a 'don't miss' attraction."

"Better," she responded quickly. "Much better. Rue Cler is the tourist version. This is the real thing."

"Thank you so much for sharing it with me," I said.

"My pleasure." And the megawatt smile. In a Parisian Bistro. Under a flawless sky, on a crisp January morning. I thought, once again, that it didn't get much better than this.

Eventually, after more observing and a little shopping, we headed back.

"There is a shortcut," Cherie said as we left the market, "it is easier for returning." She steered me down a short alley and around a corner. In front of us was a winding stairway that must have covered almost a quarter of a mile. From where we stood, it was all downhill. Which meant it would have been uphill on the way there. I was thankful that she had saved the shortcut for the return trip, and wondered whether that had been done intentionally in deference to my condition.

The stairs had to be hundreds of years old. They were chipped and worn, encrusted with ages of soil and weathered patina, but still solid and functional. Some sections had metal railings; others were wedged tightly between buildings.

As we reached the bottom of the stairway, the walls opened up into a small plaza which had a beautiful fountain as its centerpiece. As I admired the fountain, a car whizzed by, screeching to a halt not fifteen feet away. As soon as the car was stopped, the rear passenger door flew open and a man emerged, turning toward us, leaving the door open behind him. He was small, or, rather, short, but stocky, with a round, shaved head sporting a thinning layer of black stubble, and virtually no neck at all. He was clad all in black, and it took several seconds for a couple of things to register; he had on a bullet-proof vest, and he was holding a menacing-looking automatic rifle, which was pointed directly at us. I heard Cherie gasp, and felt her grab my arm.

A second later, two more men emerged from the car. One was tall and laconic in his movements. He had been the driver. He had on a white hooded sweatshirt and military-style camouflage cargo pants. He was unarmed, at least as far as I could tell, and didn't look threatening at all. The third man, jumping out of the far rear passenger seat, was instantly recognizable. There, standing before me, glaring at me across the hood of the car, dressed in jeans and a tan-colored bullet-proof vest over a green army surplus jacket, was my pickpocket.

THIRTY-FOUR

The man with the gun waved it in our direction and shouted something at us in French. Cherie pushed against me, moving us closer to the wall of the building on our right, in response to his directions. I slid the canvas bag off of my shoulder and dropped it to the ground. The driver stepped across the alley to stand against the wall of the opposing building, almost as if to distance himself from the activity in front of him. The pickpocket shut the rear door from which he'd emerged and leaned across the car, still looking at us. That's when things started to happen.

It began when the gunman took two steps forward and reached for Cherie's arm. That innocuous motion began a cascade of events that were as far from my intentions as I could have imagined.

I would like to describe my actions as heroic, paint a picture of myself as the brave citizen of the world battling the international terrorists, protecting the damsel in distress and saving the day. But it didn't go down that way, exactly. It was more like a reaction born out of sheer terror, followed by some dumb luck and physics that worked in my favor. And then the cavalry swept in.

My initial reaction was to stop the gunman from grabbing Cherie's arm, thinking that he intended to pull her toward the car. A voice in my head was screaming: "Don't let them get her into the car!" My fear caused me to reach across the guy's body without even thinking and grasp the hand that was inches from grabbing Cherie. Because I was a good six inches taller than him, the angle of my forearm as I reached forward was at about forty-five degrees downward, and the crook of my elbow snapped upward into the gun barrel as I connected with his wrist. The leverage from the impact with my arm snapped the barrel of the gun upward into his face, smashing his nose and slamming across one of his eyes. His reaction was to squeeze the trigger, releasing three quick shots up into the air which caused fiery gasses to blast from the side ports of the barrel and burn his face. All I knew at the time was that I heard him scream.

The other two men reacted in surprise at the quick series of events, with the tall one retreating into the doorway of the building where he was standing and the other, my pickpocket, starting to run first one direction, then the other, and finally freezing in place.

What happened next is not entirely clear in my mind. I know the gunman stopped reaching for Cherie's arm when the gun discharged, and my momentum carried me into her, knocking her down. I recall trying not to fall on top of her as we both hit the ground, and I know I shifted my weight slightly to the left as I caught the brunt of my fall with my left shoulder. The ensuing craziness happened outside my field of vision, as we lay on the ground, Cherie half covered by my body and me staring at the concrete beyond her right shoulder.

There were gunshots, several of them, the sound of shouting, in French, and people running. I recall wondering if any of the gunshots had been at me, and puzzling over whether I'd been shot in the back. I realized at one point that Cherie was not struggling or moving beneath me, and wondered if she had been shot.

Suddenly, all the noise and activity stopped. Things were quiet, and I found myself, once again, unable to move.

My first vivid memory after our fall came when I was able to turn my head to the right, looking past Cherie's hair, and I saw the face of the gunman, less than a foot away, slack and dead-eyed, flat against the pavement, with a pool of blood forming around his left cheek. I felt hands on me, lifting and pulling, and voices faded in from the silence. As I was being lifted upward, I remember feeling Cherie's body stir beneath me. There were a lot of men in suits hovering around in my peripheral vision, a couple of them working on getting me to my feet, and off of Cherie.

I was hoisted upright and saw Agent Bref standing in front of me. He had on a darker suit than the one he'd worn the previous day, with a white turtleneck underneath, and a black pistol hung loosely from his right hand at his side. I watched some men help Cherie up off of the ground, and felt relieved that she looked like she was all right.

"Are either of you injured?" Bref asked. I didn't immediately have an answer to his question, and I watched as Cherie moved her hands over her own arms and torso.

"I think I am fine," she said after the inspection. "I don't know. I am a little bit sore."

I realized that I was clutching my left arm tightly against my body with my right hand, and that I had pain all along my left side. "I may have hurt my arm or shoulder," I said.

Bref rattled off some instructions in French to the men around us as he slipped his gun under his jacket and into his shoulder holster. He stepped closer to where Cherie and I were standing, and led us away from the prone body of the gunman, which was literally at our feet. I slipped my good arm around Cherie's shoulders as we moved, and she grabbed me around the midsection. We hobbled that way together as Bref directed us to one of the handful of black BMWs that had seemingly appeared out of nowhere. We sat in the open doorways of the nearest car, Cherie in the front passenger seat and me in the rear, with our feet out on the street. As I gathered my wits, I was able to survey the scene in front of us.

The gunman was down on the pavement, very dead. The pool of blood around the upper part of his body had grown into an irregular oblong nearly the size of a bathtub. His gun had been scooted away from his body, leaving a bloody trail behind. The pickpocket was down on the ground, hands secured behind his back with what looked like white zip-ties. A large guy in a suit was holding him down by pushing a knee into the middle of his back. The guy in the white sweatshirt was still in the doorway, but he had slumped down onto his haunches, holding his left hand over his right shoulder, where I could see blood soaking through the sleeve of his sweatshirt. An agent in a suit had a gun pointed at his face, while a gendarme tried to examine his wound.

Bref stood by the front fender of the car, occasionally giving what sounded like supervisory directions.

"Did you shoot him?" I asked him, turning toward the front of the car.

He looked at me, hesitating slightly. "I did," he said. "When you gave me the opportunity." I must have responded with a puzzled look. "When you attacked him and took the woman down, it gave me the shot."

"How were you able to shoot him? He had on a bullet-proof vest."

"I shot him through the throat. It's one of the few vulnerable places when a target is wearing a vest. Probably hit an artery."

I thought about the distance and logistics. "You must be a good shot."

"I score adequately on the training exams. But you opened him up for me." I wondered to myself how much of an opening I had really given him, how willing he had been to put Cherie and me at risk. I didn't say anything. It didn't matter.

I glanced over at Cherie, who was listening to my exchange with Bref, her head leaned against the doorframe of the car. Her beautiful eyes were cloudy and vacant.

I looked down at the pavement. The situation felt surreal to me. It was everything I could do not to lean back on the rear seat of the car and go to sleep.

THIRTY-FIVE

The light from my desk lamp is refracted through the ice and amber liquid in the glass, throwing a rainbow-colored triangle across the surface of the desk. I am at home, in my study, a half-empty glass of scotch-on-the-rocks in front of me. I have just gotten off the phone from two calls; the first one incoming from the ER doctor to inform me that Perenzez Harris didn't make it, his injuries had been too extensive for his frail little body to withstand; the second had been outgoing, fulfilling my promise to pass the news on to Mary, the social worker. My call had awakened her, no surprise as it is three a.m., and she had simply lapsed into tears. I set the phone on the desktop, and finish most of the rest of my drink in one gulp. I lower the glass and look out the window. There is nothing but blackness outside.

"THIS IS FUCKED!" I shout, so loudly that I startle myself, dropping my fist down on the desk hard enough to rattle the ice in the glass. There is no need to worry about waking anyone, I live alone. I pour the glass nearly full of scotch from the open bottle, not bothering to replenish the ice, and stare into the brown liquid as I turn the glass slowly on the desktop. I have had my share of tragedy in my life. I am not unaccustomed to dealing with grief, guilt, anger and frustration. For some reason, however, the cruel, violent death of this little boy for whom I was supposed to be legally responsible, has sucker-punched me like nothing I can recall. This seems to be such a personal loss, but that makes no sense. Two years earlier, I hadn't even known P existed.

I swallow some more scotch, letting the subtle burn languish on the back of my tongue. I know it won't help, but it sure as hell can't hurt. I flip open my laptop and click on the internet explorer. I go to an airfare website and enter all the necessary data to find one-way flights for various European destinations over the coming two-to-three-week period. The machine does its thing, quietly whirring and clicking as it reaches into the ether for information.

As I wait for the screen to update, I feel the nudge of a blocky head against my leg, beneath the desk. I know it is the black dog. I listen to his quiet panting in the darkness, smell the dank odor of his thick coat. His ropey tail thumps against the desk, his claws click quietly on the wood floor as he shifts his weight from foot to foot. I reach down to stroke his broad head, but he is gone, leaving behind only the impression of dampness from his jowls on my pant leg.

I hear a "ding" and see the screen of my phone light up, the email icon appearing on the display. I push the icon without picking up the phone, and the message fills the rectangular screen. It is from Patty: "Can't sleep, know you can't either. Sorry about your kiddo, that's a tough one. Hang in there." I close the message and sip some more scotch. I shut my eyes and lower my head to rest it against my forearm on the desk. I want to stay that way forever.

THIRTY-SIX

An ambulance showed up after about ten minutes, and Bref made sure that Cherie and I were the first ones attended to. Since it didn't look like either of us would need a gurney or life support, they loaded us together into the back, where we sat on padded benches facing each other. One of the EMTs wrapped a Velcro contraption around my torso and left arm, cinching it tight, which essentially immobilized my entire left arm and shoulder.

I reached across the open middle section, where a gurney would usually be situated, with my untethered arm and took Cherie's hand in mine. "I'm sorry I got you into this," I said, searching her eyes for a clue as to how she was feeling.

"Not your fault," she said in response. "How could you have known?" She squeezed my hand. "And we're both okay." Her expression was still vacant.

We were quiet the rest of the way to the hospital. I noticed that the ambulance didn't have the siren going, and wondered if we at least warranted the flashing lights.

The ambulance backed into the hospital emergency bay, and the EMTs helped us out of the vehicle and into the receiving area of the emergency room, where they handed us off to nurses and orderlies that began checking us in. Cherie glanced my direction and I overheard her tell one of the nurses something that included the word "*Anglais*", and I assumed she was informing them that I didn't speak French, because in short order I had a male nurse attending to me who spoke passable English.

"We will do the x-ray," he said, pointing to my arm, "to make sure no broken bones." I nodded in agreement and he whisked me off into an x-ray room and turned me over to the tech who ran the machine. They didn't remove my Velcro wrap, but shot the x-rays right through it, which made me happy. The less messing with my arm, the less pain. When they were done shooting radiation through me, the nurse took me back and parked me in a curtained cubicle, with the end open toward the Emergency Room itself. The cubicles formed a circle around the center island, where the main nurse's station was located. I looked around the circle to see if I could find Cherie. I spied her at about three o'clock to my seven o'clock on the circle. I tried to make eye contact, but couldn't get her attention.

I spotted Gregor as soon as he stepped into the ER, towering over the medical workers in their blue scrubs. He scanned all the cubicles, and didn't see me, but zeroed in on Cherie right away. He lumbered over to her cubicle, where she was sitting on the bed with her legs dangling over the side.

I could see them talking. Gregor seemed concerned; Cherie was dismissive. A doctor showed up to examine Cherie, and Gregor slipped out of the cubicle as the doctor pulled the curtain over the opening.

Gregor looked around, then headed my way when he saw me.

"You look a mess," he said as he approached.

"You should see the other guy," I said. He just stared at me. "American humor," I said, by way of explanation.

"How are you injured?"

"I did something to my arm or shoulder. To tell you the truth, I haven't even tried to move it since they put this splint on it in the ambulance. I'm a little afraid to."

"They have good doctors here; they will take care of it." He stuffed his hands into his pockets. "Bref tells me you probably saved Cherie's life."

"I think that's a little dramatic. I did no such thing."

"Bref's been around the block a time or two. If he says it, I believe him."

I didn't know what to say to that. I did, however, see an opening that I would be stupid not to take advantage of.

"Gregor," I said, "just exactly what has been going on with all this? How did those guys find me?"

Gregor looked very uncomfortable. I could tell he was considering where his loyalties should lie. "First of all," he started, "I never imagined Cherie would be involved in any way." He let that hang there for a second. "And I really can only tell you what I suspect, because Malboeuf never included me in any details. He used me, as well as you."

I sensed that I would get further by just letting him run with it, so I kept on quietly looking at him.

"I pretty much figured it out when Malboeuf questioned me about our chasing that one suspect, the one you said was your pickpocket. He asked me if I thought the guy had gotten a good look at you, if I thought he recognized you."

"Do you think he did?"

"I saw him look back at you. There wasn't much doubt in my mind that he knew who you were."

"And you told Malboeuf that?"

"Yes. And then Bref came into the picture. I know him only by reputation. He's what we would call a 'specialist'. He usually runs surveillance and protection operations. He's not just a field agent. He's a sanctioned operator."

"I don't understand. You mean like 'license to kill' and all that?"

"Well, not exactly. He can run an operation. He can set it all up so that he can spring a trap."

I let that sink in for several seconds. "And I was the bait?"

"More or less. Yes."

I thought about how all those black BMWs, guys in suits and uniformed gendarmes had shown up so quickly in that obscure little plaza. It all made sense. The only logical explanation was that Bref had been lurking in the background, ready to "spring his trap".

"That whole trip with Bref, delivering you to Cherie's house, was nothing but a reconnaissance run for him," he said, as if in response to what I was thinking. "He was setting up his operation."

"But how did the terrorists find me?" I asked. "Surely Malboeuf didn't have anything to do with that."

"He didn't need to. They found you the same way Malboeuf found you to begin with. Probably more easily; remember, they had all your personal information. These groups are great with the internet, run circles around the police."

"And that led them right to Cherie's house. You had to have figured that out."

He rubbed a big hand over his face, anxiety permeating his countenance.

"I took a calculated risk," he said. "I had to weigh my getting involved and risking my job against the danger to Cherie. I was pretty sure they wouldn't do anything at the house, hoping that they wouldn't do anything at all. I certainly wasn't counting on her being with you when they did."

"It was all pretty much of a longshot, wasn't it?"

"Yes, but Malboeuf was under a lot of pressure. He was willing to bet on longshots."

"Well, I guess his bet paid off. It seems to me that Malboeuf is a cold, calculating bastard."

Gregor thought about that. It was clear that he didn't disagree, but equally clear that he was not quick to jump on board with my assessment. "It's all very complicated," he said, finally. "As I told you before, this whole thing is a very big deal, to Paris and all of France. Malboeuf has that all resting on his shoulders."

I noticed that he had couched his response in the form of an explanation, not an excuse or apology. Maybe I had underestimated Gregor again. Maybe he was more than a big oaf of a policeman. The position he had maintained in this whole affair had been very cleverly more diplomatic and self-preserving than I would have expected from him. Once again, I was sure those instincts had served him well in reaching his position.

I saw Cherie out of the corner of my eye, mobile, out of her cubicle and headed our direction. "Let's keep this between us, Gregor," I said tilting my head in Cherie's direction.

Gregor turned and saw her approaching. "I agree," he said quietly, nodding at me.

THIRTY-SEVEN

"**A**re you okay?" I asked Cherie as she stepped into my cubicle.

"The doctor has cleared me," she said. "I have only some minor scrapes and bruises. I am released."

I breathed a sigh of relief. Gregor nodded his approval.

"How about you?" she asked.

"They took an x-ray of my arm," I said. "I haven't heard from them since."

As if on cue, a doctor in green scrubs pushed a portion of the curtain aside and stepped around Gregor to stand next to my bed.

"Monsieur McCann?" he asked, looking at the chart in his hand.

"Yes?" I replied.

"We have read your x-ray, and do not see any fractures, other than a very old one, probably a childhood injury. You most likely have a partial separation in your shoulder, and I will want to look at that." He stepped closer, put down the chart and began unwrapping me from the Velcro device. I helped him out, turning and bending so he could pull it all the way off. Surprisingly, the pain wasn't excruciating. He poked around my shoulder, lifting my arm upward by the elbow. When it reached an angle of about sixty degrees, I winced in pain, leaning away from him.

"Ugh," I said. "That hurts."

"Yes," he said. "We will put you into a sling, but I don't think we will need to do any more than that. And I will prescribe some pain medication." He glanced up at my forehead. "And this occurred at the same time?" he asked, pointing toward the bandage.

"No," I said, touching my fingers to the gauze. "I already had this."

"But we would like you to take a look at it," Cherie chimed in. "It wasn't properly treated, and I think it may need to be sutured." The doctor looked at her. "I am a nurse," she said, as if that explained everything.

"I see," the doctor said, reaching up to pull at the tape securing the bandage. "Let's just have a look, then." He pulled the tape and gauze off carefully and pushed and squeezed at the wound in much the same way Cherie had done at her house. "Hmm. I think you may be correct. I think several sutures might be in order. I will have a nurse get with you for that."

"And one more thing," Cherie said, not at all meekly. "He has been having difficulty breathing for the last week. He seems to have a bronchitis or such. I'm afraid it might progress to pneumonia."

"Hmm," the doctor said, taking his stethoscope from around his neck. "Let's have a listen." He placed the stethoscope against my back and the earpieces into his ears. "Breathe deeply, please." I did so, as much as I could. I was reluctant to tell him that I really hadn't been able to do that for several days. "Again." I repeated the effort.

He switched the stethoscope around to my chest and said: "Breathe normally." He changed location several times, and listened at the final spot for an extremely long time. He had a look of deep concentration on his face, like he was trying to block out all the noise and activity around us. He moved the stethoscope an inch to the right and listened some more. He pulled the scope away, stood up straight, and poked around on my neck. "Lay flat, please," he said, so I did. He pushed on my belly, and then pulled up one of my pant legs and prodded at my lower leg and ankle several times. He took a half step back from the bed and said: "Monsieur McCann, I am going to order some tests for you. You can stay right here for now, but you will be taken upstairs for the tests."

"What tests?" I asked, sitting up and glancing at Cherie.

"An EKG and echocardiogram to begin with. Those will help me determine whether what I am hearing is of concern or not. Neither are painful, and will only take a little time. Once we have those results, we will go from there. And we will have some blood drawn. Any questions?"

"What exactly is it that you're hearing?" I asked.

He hesitated, thinking. "I'm not sure it's of great concern, but what I hear in your heartbeat is a slight irregularity. As if the rhythm were offbeat." He paused, probably searching for the English words to quantify his observations. "In my off-duty time I am a musician," he went on, waving his stethoscope absently, "so indulge me in my example. What I normally hear from a heart is a steady beat: pah-boom, pah-boom, pah-boom. Yours is not so steady, like syncopation in music: pah-da-boom, pah-da-boom, da-boom." He poked at the air with his finger, in time with his pah-da-booms.

"Like a heart murmur?" I asked, thinking I had the idea.

"Not exactly," he said. "That is why I want to run the tests. To see if we can figure out what this abnormal rhythm is telling us." He paused; his finger still poised in the air. "Anything else?"

I looked at Cherie and she gave me a shrug. "I guess not," I said.

"Okay, then, I will see you later on, after the tests." He whipped the stethoscope around his neck, picked up my chart and walked out of the cubicle, toward the center station.

I looked at Cherie again. "Should I be concerned?"

"I don't know," she said. "I think he just wants to check it out. Probably just an abundance of caution."

I nodded. Didn't know what else to do at that point.

"Um, sorry," Gregor said softly. "I need to go. Cherie, I can give you a ride home."

Cherie looked at him like he was a puppy that had just pissed on the floor. "I'm not going anywhere," she said.

Gregor took a step away from us, hesitated, then took another step and stopped. He looked at Cherie, then at me. "Alright, then, I'll be off." He strode directly to the ER exit and through the door.

Cherie walked over to the side of the bed and took my hand.

A young girl with glasses in a set of blue scrubs came in almost immediately and began explaining her presence in French. Cherie conversed with her, and then informed me that she was going to draw some blood from my arm. "Left or right?" Cherie asked.

I raised my right arm toward the girl, as my left one was still pretty sore, and she went to work, deftly filling four vials with blood in less than a minute. She gathered up the vials and her equipment and exited the cubicle, giving us a polite smile on the way out.

In several minutes an orderly in maroon scrubs pulled up to the cubicle pushing a wheelchair. He looked at a clipboard. "Monsieur McCann?" he asked.

I nodded, and he rattled off a barrage of French that Cherie once again handled on my behalf. I wondered to myself how I would have navigated the ordeal without her.

"Hop in," she said, pointing at the wheelchair. "You're going for a ride."

I slid off of the bed and into the chair, a little surprised at how unsteady and weak I was. "You're coming with me, aren't you?" I asked Cherie.

"Of course," she said, running her hand through the back of my hair and down onto my neck. I reached up and put my hand on top of hers. She gave me a little squeeze and the orderly steered me toward a hallway leading off the side of the ER to a bank of elevators. We rolled into an open elevator, the doors slid shut, the orderly punched the button for the third floor and we began rising silently upward.

THIRTY-EIGHT

The bedside clock projects a glow of green into the darkness of the room. Three-seventeen a.m. I roll over and stare at the numbers until they change. Three-eighteen a.m. This is the biggest adjustment for me since Patty has been gone. I simply cannot seem to make the transition to sleeping alone in the seemingly enormous bed. I have doubled my dosage of antidepressant medication, which is supposed to have the side effect of making me tired, spend nearly three hours at the gym each evening, and eat good, healthy foods that should not interfere with sleep. Yet I watch the green numbers change for hours at a time.

I can never seem to get the temperature quite right. I experiment with the heat, the air conditioning, opening and closing windows, setting up fans. I can't find that elusive comfort zone which will allow me to sleep. Maybe it's the subtle effect of that other body being absent from the bed. The difference created by removing a constant 98.6-degree heat source. I look at the clock. Three-nineteen a.m.

The phone rings on the bedside table, startling me. It's the land line, attached to an old corded phone. I slide over on the bed and pick up the handset, answering: "Hello?" There is no response. I say "hello" again, but hear only the hiss of the open line. I lower the handset softly back onto its cradle, flipping the cord out of the way with a practiced motion of my wrist. I settle my head back onto the pillow, level with the green numbers of the clock. Three-twenty a.m.

THIRTY-NINE

The tests were non-invasive, painless and not too annoying, so long as you don't mind having electrodes attached to your chest and goopy gel smeared all over your torso. None of the technicians commented on any of the results, and Cherie didn't exchange more than a handful of words with them, mostly about where they wanted me to sit, lay down or wait. She stayed right by my side, as much as some of the cramped quarters allowed, and asked me, as each procedure ended, if I had any questions. I didn't. Didn't know enough to ask any.

We didn't return to the ER, but went to a room on the fifth floor. The orderly left me there, sitting in the wheelchair in my street clothes, with no further instructions. Cherie shrugged at my inquisitive look. "I guess we wait here," she said. She sat down in the chair against the wall at the foot of the empty bed, crossed her legs and began bouncing her foot up and down. After a few minutes, a nurse came in, verified my identity, put my left arm into a blue sling, tightened it up just beyond comfortable and then went to work on my head. She talked with Cherie in French throughout the process, and I assumed that some of it was an explanation as to what she was doing. After she shot a local anesthetic into my forehead, I didn't feel much, but Cherie informed me that she closed up my gash with ten or so sutures, and that she had done a very good job of it. The injury was covered back up with a bandage before I had a chance see it, so I had to take her word for it.

After the nurse left, I got up out of the wheelchair just to move around, and Cherie asked me several times if I was feeling okay. I stepped out into the hallway once, and there was no one visible in either direction. I went back into the room and resumed my seat.

After about forty-five minutes, my ER doctor walked through the open door, followed by another doctor wearing a white lab coat over his scrubs.

"Sorry for your wait," the ER doctor said. Cherie and I both nodded in acknowledgement. "This is Dr. Patek," he went on, pointing toward the other doctor. "He will be your cardiologist. I'm going to let him explain your test results."

Dr. Patek stepped forward. He was tiny in stature, dark-skinned, dark-haired and dark-eyed, and I assumed that he was East Indian. He extended a hand to me as I sat in the wheelchair. "Mister McCann," he said in a sharp British accent, "very pleased to meet you."

"Likewise," I said, shaking his hand. It was soft and delicate, almost feminine.

He hesitated slightly, and went on: "I have read your tests and reviewed your lab work, and it would appear that you are in congestive heart failure." He paused for a second, giving me time to recover from the punch to the gut that some phantom slugger in the room had just landed. I wasn't aware of Cherie's movement from the chair to where I was parked, but I felt her hand on my shoulder.

"What this means," Dr. Patek continued, "is that your heart muscle is weakened and is not effectively pumping blood to the rest of your body. We will need to determine why this is happening, and the extent to which your heart has been damaged. Do you understand?"

"Sure," I said. "Is that why I've had trouble breathing?"

"Yes, when your heart is not working efficiently, it tries to compensate by beating harder and faster, which causes several things to happen. One of those things is for your body to retain fluids, particularly in the space around your heart, and this fluid can restrict your lungs from being able to fully expand. You experience this as shortness of breath. Have you had any chest or arm pain associated with the breathing problems?"

"No," I said, thinking back. I couldn't recall anything that felt like a heart problem.

"That is good. It would indicate that the cause of this heart weakness is not likely a heart attack, which is consistent with your initial bloodwork. We will be doing some further tests to see if we can figure out what is causing it. The first thing we need to do is put you on an IV diuretic which will help your body to begin expelling that retained fluid. Right now, your Ejection Fraction, or 'EF', is between fifteen and twenty percent. This number measures the efficiency of your heart in moving blood out to the rest of the body. Hopefully, as we get the fluid off, your EF will increase."

"Okay, so what's 'normal', what is this EF number supposed to be?"

"It varies from individual to individual, and with age, but the normal range for someone like you would be fifty-five to seventy."

"Huh," I said, expressing some surprise. "I guess I have a way to go."

He looked at me with concern. "You need to understand that you have damage to your heart, and most likely will never be back up to 'normal' levels. What we have to do now is determine what we can do to allow you to get as much improvement as possible."

"I understand what you're saying," I said. "I'm a good healer. Tell me what to do and we'll get working on it."

"The first thing we will do is admit you to the hospital, and start you on those drugs I mentioned. The next thing in order would be a heart catheterization."

He looked back and forth from me to Cherie. "Do you understand everything I've told you?" It was as if he was expecting a more dramatic reaction, or that he was afraid we didn't understand the gravity of the situation.

Cherie stepped around behind my wheelchair and moved both hands down over my chest, almost protectively. I reached up and squeezed her arm. "Yes," I said, "I think we get it."

Dr. Patek handed me back over to the ER doctor, who in turn passed me off to a nurse that took me to a different floor and into another room. She went through all the information and paperwork necessary to get me admitted, and we waded our way as best we could through the tricky insurance part. I had been assured before I began my trip that my U.S. insurance should cover this sort of hospitalization, but truly didn't know for sure that it would. Once the paperwork was finished, a floor nurse took over and got me into a hospital gown, which was no easy task given the sling on my arm, and into the bed. In short order, another young girl in blue scrubs showed up and put an IV in my arm. The floor nurse hung a clear bag of liquid from a bedside stand and started the drip into my IV. I asked if I could have anything for the pain in my shoulder and head, and Cherie translated to the nurse for me. She came back with two white pills in a tiny paper cup and handed me a glass of water to take them with. I did so.

The room was pretty much the same as a hospital room in the U.S., except with more tile. There was tile on the floors, on the walls all the way to the ceiling, and even tile on the ceiling of the bathroom. Probably a sterile environment, anti-germ kind of thing. Any surface that wasn't tile seemed to be stainless steel. I had a small window that looked out onto a parking lot, and two visitor's chairs; one a large, comfortable-looking recliner next to the bed for guests intending to stay a while, and the other a very hard, angular chrome-and-plastic number in the corner for those who would be in and out very quickly.

When the activity seemed to have subsided, I turned to Cherie, who had taken up a position in the big chair on the far side of my bed. "You didn't sign on for this," I said. "You don't need to stay. I'm sure they will take very good care of me."

She reached up from the chair and placed her hand on my forearm, moving it back and forth lightly. "I'm not going anywhere," she said. Again.

FORTY

I *am visualizing my emotional psyche. It is an exercise as-signed by Bob, my therapist. My visualization isn't very sophisticated, actually it's quite adolescent. It is a big valentine heart, in the Chuck Jones cartoon style. In the aftermath of Patty, it lays broken into a thousand little pieces, smashed by a giant hammer. Envision a cartoon character, wielding a big wooden-handled sledgehammer, sneaking out from behind a cartoon-landscape rock and giving it a good overhand whack, and the resulting "kapow" impact, with jagged, fiery lines and smoke plumes. And then the resulting debris, tiny fragments of quivering red gel-like pieces, strewn across the cartoon landscape, trying desperately to reformulate themselves into their original composition. But mostly just lying there, useless and dysfunctional, quivering away in a helpless state, waiting on a stimulus, or a force, to reconstruct them into a useful and functioning organ. I am embarrassed to imagine how this amateurish depiction will sound to Bob. Maybe I'll come up with a better one before our next session.*

FORTY-ONE

I needed to let my daughter know what was going on, so I had Cherie retrieve my phone from of the bag of clothing and other personal effects that had been stowed in a cabinet in my hospital room. I considered calling, but did the time computation and figured out that it was still before five a.m. in Portland. In addition, it looked like my phone battery was just about dead, and I knew that a conversation would eat up most of the juice it had left, so I sent a text. Short, sweet, to the point.

"I need a couple things, if you don't mind," I said to Cherie, after I had sent the text. "I need my phone charger. It's plugged into the outlet by the bed, at your house. I also need my meds and other stuff that's in my Dopp kit, right on top of my back-pack. Just bring the whole kit."

"Okay," she said. "Anything else?"

"Yeah, maybe those boxers that are laying on the bed. I think they'll let me wear them under this gown."

"Are you shy?" she asked, grinning at me.

"No," I replied, chuckling. "It just feels weird."

"Okay. I'll be back in a bit. I'm guessing an hour or so by Metro."

"Take a cab, I'd be happy to pay for it."

"Oh, no. The Metro will be faster. I almost never use cabs."

"Alright, whatever works best for you. Thanks."

She reached over the footboard of the bed and squeezed my foot through the sheets. "No thanks are needed. I am here for you." She winked, pivoted on her toes and marched out the door with a smile on her face. What had I done to get so lucky?

My phone rang almost immediately. I answered it on the first ring.

"DAD!" It was Lauren. "What the hell?"

"It's no big deal, Lauren, I'm okay."

"You send me a text to tell me you're in the hospital in France? What the hell is that?"

"I thought you guys texted everything, that you never make calls."

"Well, I'm making one now. Are you alright?"

"I'm fine, I'm fine. They're just running some tests."

"Yeah, sure Dad, I know you. If you're sitting in a hospital room, it's pretty fuckin' serious."

"It's not *that* serious, and who taught you how to swear like that?"

"I think you know the answer to that. I'm booking a flight right now; I'll be there tomorrow afternoon."

"Lauren, you don't need to do that. You don't need to come."

"Shut up. I'm coming."

"Who'll watch the kids?"

"Jeff has family leave he can take. This is exactly what it's for."

I didn't have the energy to argue with her. And I knew from many years of experience that it would be pointless to do so, anyway.

"What exactly is wrong?" she asked.

"It's just a little thing with my heart, no big deal. I'll give you all the details when you get here. And my phone's about to die."

I could tell that she wasn't satisfied with my answer. I could also hear her typing on her computer in the background. "Damn," she said, "gettin' to France ain't cheap." I was thankful for the distraction.

"I'll pay for your ticket," I said.

"You bet you will. See you tomorrow. And Dad?"

"What Peanut?"

"Just concentrate on getting well. I love you."

"I love you too. Have a safe flight."

Not ten minutes after I hung up the phone, I heard the email ding. The message read: "I understand you're in the hospital and Lauren's on her way. I'm sure she'll take good care of you. Be a good patient, and don't piss off the doctors. Take care. Patty." Bad news travels fast.

I had visits from several nurses, whose collective English was very limited, and I found myself missing my trusty interpreter. We muddled through it without too much confusion. One of them was there to stick electrodes on me and hook me up to a box on a pole to monitor my vital signs and who-knows-what-else. I was pleased to discover that the whole contraption worked on Bluetooth, or something like it, so that I wouldn't have a second thing tethering me. The transmitter slipped into a pocket in the front of my gown, and the leads ran to my body through an internal opening. Pretty slick, leaving me to deal with only the IV.

I found an English-language news channel on the television and, for the first time, came to fully understand the gravity of the *Charlie Hebdo* situation in Paris. I realized that I'd had no idea of everything that was going on during my limited, frantic involvement. It was disconcerting to see some familiar scenes show up on the screen, and at one point I almost expected to see video of myself, but such wasn't the case. I noticed that the latest event, our experience with Bref and the shoot-out in the little plaza, had not yet made the news. Maybe it wouldn't. Gregor had me thinking that anything involving Agent Bref would be shrouded in layers of mystery and deception.

There appeared to be one suspect still at large, a woman. They were playing things close to the vest until she was captured. Or killed. One thing was clear from the coverage; the people of Paris were afraid, angry, affronted. They were not going to tolerate that kind of violence in their city, on their turf. Their support of the victims was inspiring, rallying around the slogan "*Je suis Charlie*": "I am Charlie." I found myself silently chanting with them.

When Cherie returned with my stuff, I was still watching the news coverage.

"Turn that off," she said. "I've had too much of it. It makes me crazy."

Just as I complied with her request, Dr. Patek walked in. "Good afternoon," he said. "How are you feeling?"

"As good as ever," was my reply, and it was nearly the truth. This heart ailment had crept up on me in such a gradual way that I didn't fully realize how bad I was feeling. The painkillers had kicked in, so my head and shoulder had stopped hurting. I was good.

"That's a good sign," he said, looking at my chart. "It looks like we haven't started to get that fluid off yet. Have the nurses explained that we want to keep track of your urine output?" I must have given him a confused look, because he stepped into the bathroom and came out with what looked like a big plastic pitcher. "You will urinate into this, and then let the nurse know. They will measure and dispose of it." One of the nurses had probably explained that to me, I just hadn't understood.

"I can do that," I said, but I was looking at the pitcher and wondering how I would accomplish the feat one-handed.

"We are going to be doing a heart catheterization first thing in the morning," he went on. "We will insert a small tube called a cardiac catheter into a vein in your arm and run it all the way into your heart. It will allow us to perform some tests on your heart's function, and on the blood vessels that supply your heart, so that we can determine what may be causing this weakened condition. Many doctors do this procedure with the patient awake, but I prefer to put you under a light anesthesia, if that is okay with you."

"Fine by me," I said. Honestly, the idea of being awake

while they threaded a tube all the way from my arm into my heart didn't appeal much to me.

Cherie and I spent the rest of the evening watching a series of game shows on TV, with the sound off and the closed captioning on. The closed captioning was in French, but it didn't matter, we weren't really paying attention. We were both dozing, in and out, Cherie in the chair and me in the bed.

The nurses came and went, doing their nursing thing. One of them had several medications for me to start on, in pill form. I had her explain it all to Cherie, who said they were heart medications, and that she would give me the details later.

At some point I told Cherie to go home and get some rest. Her response was to get a blanket out of the cabinet and curl up in the chair. I didn't argue with her. It had been a very long day. A very long week.

It was a fitful night. Anyone whose been there can tell you how difficult it is to get a good night's sleep in a hospital. The TV stayed on, and the nurses were in and out at least hourly. The monitors made unfamiliar noises and emitted strange, unnatural lights, and the diuretic they were pumping into my system sent me to the bathroom on a regular basis. Cherie tossed and turned in her chair, trying to get comfortable. Later, in the depths of the night, after the activity had subsided, I lay there on my back, unable to move, frozen in place not by the sling, the IV, or the heart monitor, but by anxiety.

FORTY-TWO

*I*t is cold and rainy in Portland, as it is much of the time during this part of the year. I am huddled beneath a green canvas tent with a half dozen other people at a run-down cemetery in one of the older parts of town. We are listening as a minister who never knew him says a few words about Perenzez Harris before they bury him. The size of the casket only adds to the tragic mood that permeates the tent. The plain wooden box is only about four feet long, and sits precariously atop the mechanical scaffold, designed to hold a full-size coffin, which is set up above the gravesite. I see no one that I can identify as P's family, and recognize all but a couple of the people present as being involved in his court case in one way or another. The minister finishes his brief service and people filter out from under the canvas, opening their umbrellas as they leave. I nod to Mary, the social worker, as she walks by.

Bob, my therapist, sidles up next to me, and I give him a look of surprise. "Did you know P?" I ask.

"No," he replies, "but I talked to your office and they said you'd be here."

"Well, I'm glad you came. Added one more person to a small crowd."

"You canceled your appointments for the next few weeks."

"Yeah, I'm going to be doing a little traveling, and I'll be really busy wrapping up cases and getting things squared away with my clients."

"Your assistant Meredith says you're going to be out of

the office indefinitely. That you've got someone lined up to take things over for you. That sounds like more than 'a little traveling', Michael."

"Yeah, well, it's an open-ended trip. I'm not sure when I'll be back, and it's not fair to anyone to leave things hanging."

"You think you'll find some answers in Europe?"

"Oh, so Meredith told you."

"I'm pretty good at getting information out of people. So where to in Europe?"

I sigh. I'm not really ready to discuss this with anyone, least of all my therapist. "I've got a one-way ticket for Brussels. I leave in three weeks. From there, I don't really have a plan."

We both watch in silence as the cemetery workers remove the draping and flowers from around the casket and begin cranking on the scaffold to lower little P into the ground. We watch until the casket has reached the bottom of the grave, and they begin removing the supporting straps.

"Let's walk," Bob says. "You can share my umbrella." He opens up a black umbrella and we set out among the memorial markers toward the last two cars still parked along the paved cemetery road. We bump shoulders awkwardly as we both lean into the shelter of the umbrella. We stop at the front fender of his car, a blue Volvo wagon. "Are you doing okay?" he asks.

"Sure," I say. I haven't told him about my latest visit from the black dog. Contrary to popular belief, you don't always tell your therapist everything.

"Take care," he says, extending his hand. "I'm available by phone, anytime. And I can pre-write prescriptions for you, or fax them to pharmacies wherever you are."

"I appreciate that," I say. "I'll be in touch." I shake his hand and watch as he gets into his car and drives away.

The rain is cold as it runs down the back of my neck and under my coat collar. I look back toward the gravesite and see a couple of the workers taking down the tent. Another one of them starts up a backhoe that is parked a discreet distance away, shattering the silence and drowning out the patter of the rain, steering it toward the gaping hole in the ground. As I step around to the far side of my car and open the door, I can see the battered yellow bucket of the machine bite into the pile of freshly-disturbed earth and move it toward the grave.

FORTY-THREE

The morning brought a flurry of activity. The heart catheterization people showed up at the crack of dawn. They told Cherie she should wait in the room, then took me down to an operating arena, shaved and prepped my arm, gave me another IV, kissed me goodnight and put me to sleep.

Immediately, I was somewhere else, removed from all the activity, hovering around in my subconscious. I was still trying to make sense of it all. It seemed like everything had happened so fast. These situations are supposed to take years to develop. You get old, start complaining about your aches and pains, have trouble getting to the gym and compare health problems with your friends. You get heartburn, diverticulitis, arthritis and gum disease, maybe have a knee or hip replaced. You tell the same story ten times, and people around you roll their eyes. Your kids think you're a burden, even if they never say it. You are someone very different from me.

I meandered around Pity Town for a while, then hiked over to Realityville. I spent some time exploring things there, and found a spot where I felt pretty comfortable, a place that I could set up camp. I eventually came to a grudging peace with this affliction which had visited itself upon me, and with the fate that it would dictate. I had always been a fighter by nature, whether it was in a courtroom, in a sports competition, or protecting the ones I love, and I wasn't inclined to change my stripes. You give it your best shot and accept the outcome, no regrets.

I awoke from a hazy unconsciousness to find another

woman in my bed. Well, technically, this one was a repeat. Cherie had nestled herself into the impossibly small space between my body and the railing of the hospital bed, her head against my shoulder, her slender hand resting lightly on the center of my chest.

"Hello, there," I said. My voice sounded strange and far away. "Haven't we met like this before?"

She stirred by my side, raising her head to where I could see her clearly. She was still dressed in her running gear from the day before, sans shoes. I kind of missed the flimsy night-shirt. "I believe we have. How are you feeling?"

"Much better *now*."

"I wanted to be right here when you woke up."

"I'm glad you were."

We were quiet for a while. Truth is, I sort of faded in and out. It was very comfortable, like drifting along on a lavender-scented cloud. I recall being surprised that the nurses stayed away for so long. Maybe Cherie had bribed them.

"Michael," Cherie said, finally breaking the silence, "I have a question for you."

"Shoot." No joke intended.

"Do you think this is going anywhere?"

More silence, but I was no longer drifting in and out. She had my full attention.

"I don't know," I said, finally. "First, there's all this stuff with my heart. That's a little overwhelming at this point. And then the logistics are intimidating. An international relationship? I never planned to meet anyone while I was over here, haven't really even had time to think about what that might mean." I paused, considering my words carefully. "And I'm just a little uncomfortable with the whole Gregor thing."

Her turn for silence. It went on long enough for it to become a little uncomfortable. "So, am I just going to have to love you from afar? Is that what they say?" Her breath was soft against the side of my neck.

"Well, you're not very afar right now."

Her fingers raised up and then popped me on the sternum, playfully. "You know what I mean." She rubbed my chest, as if to apologize for the little tap.

I sighed. "I do," I said.

We were quiet for a little longer. I felt like she was waiting for me to say more. I searched desperately among the scattered pieces of my busted-up cartoon heart. They were moving, merging, reassembling, but they were still in disarray. I tried to stack them up, shovel them into piles, super glue them together, find some way to make them functional again. Try as I might, I couldn't come up with any sort of reconstruction, or with anything to say to Cherie.

"Well, then," she said, pressing her forehead into my neck, "I'll just have to make the most of this time we have." I slipped my arm under her shoulder, kissing her lightly on the top of her head as I did so. She nestled in closer, if that was possible.

It was a very nice little interlude, but of course it couldn't last forever. This was a hospital, after all. A nurse came in, checked my chart, gave us an amused look and adjusted the flow valve of my IV bag. She said something to Cherie in French, and Cherie responded with a sly smile.

"She wants to know if you need anything," Cherie whispered in my ear. I had my doubts about the accuracy of the translation.

"No, I'm good," I said. "In fact, if I were any better it would probably be illegal, even in France."

Cherie gazed up at me with soft eyes. She gave my status report to the nurse, who smiled and left the room.

I felt bad about the obviously mixed signals I was giving Cherie, but I was truly in a very confusing place. I was waging an inner struggle of immense proportions with myself and both of my hearts, the physical and emotional, both damaged and of uncertain health or future. I felt like I should apologize. I still couldn't find the words.

A few minutes later, the door swung open cautiously with a small accompanying knock, and Miranda stuck her head into the room. She had evidently come all the way from Bonn to see me. Or at least that's what I chose to assume.

"Come on in," I said. She came out from behind the door, smiling. She stopped short when she saw Cherie.

"Good God, Mother. It's a hospital."

"I'm well aware of that, Miranda dear. I'm a nurse, and I am watching over my patient."

"It's embarrassing, Mother. What if one of the real nurses came in?"

"I would begin administering CPR." She didn't tell her that we'd crossed that bridge already.

"God, you're hopeless."

Dr. Patek followed closely on Miranda's heels, and Cherie extricated herself from her narrow perch when he walked in, without any apology or embarrassment.

"Good morning, Mister McCann," he said. "I trust our procedure did not cause too much discomfort."

"Not a bit," I said.

"Well," he went on, "we found nothing of import from the heart cath. No blockages, no constricted vessels, nothing that needs to be addressed by surgery. You have what is referred to as idiopathic cardiomyopathy, meaning 'without known cause'."

"Okay," I said, "so we know what it's not. Do we know what it is?"

The doctor twisted his mouth and spread his hands to his sides in a surrendering gesture, my chart in his right, a pen in the left. "Most likely a virus or an infection caused this. Given the progressive stage, I'd say whatever it might have been was a long time in your system."

"Do we run tests for it?"

"No, we treat whatever remains and go forward from here."

"So, we'll never know?"

"In all likelihood, no. We'll focus on getting you better, try to determine how much permanent damage your heart has sustained."

"How are we doing on that front?"

"We measured your EF again during the cath procedure. There's been no real change. Yet. Which concerns me. As long as your heart function is in this low range, you are at risk of your heart stopping suddenly. Of course, we are monitoring that, but you need to be aware of that possibility. This is a condition which may or may not persist, we simply don't know at this point. We need to let the medications do their work, and continue to get this fluid out of your system. I'll check back with you later. In the meantime, rest." He turned abruptly and headed for the door, waving at us with the chart as he departed. "Remember, rest!"

"Do you see those boxers I was wearing?" I asked Cherie after he had left the room.

She delivered them, and I clumsily maneuvered into them one-handed beneath the sheets.

"Thanks," I said. "I have no idea why, but they made me take them off for the procedure. I figured the least I could do is not make Miranda have to look at my bare arse."

"Oh, I'm accustomed to missing underwear," Miranda said from her chair in the corner. She smiled mischievously.

"Your phone dinged while the doctor was here," Cherie said, motioning toward the tray by the bed, ignoring Miranda.

"Thanks," I said again. I pulled my phone off the charger and checked the new email message.

"Lauren is held up in London," it said. "She'll be late, but you know our daughter, she will be there, hell or high water. Take care. Patty."

"It looks like my daughter is stuck in London for the time being," I said.

"I hope I still get to meet her," Miranda said. Cherie nodded.

"Oh, she'll get here. Believe me, even if she has to rent a rowboat to cross the Channel, she'll get here. Lauren is very," I paused to find the right word, "determined. No... 'forceful' is more like it." They both laughed.

I was still staring at the phone, reviewing the message. I must have had a look of annoyance, amusement or confusion on my face.

"What?" Cherie asked, looking at me. "Does she say more?"

"No, no," I said dismissively, "the message wasn't actually from her. It was from the kids' mother. She's been keeping pretty close tabs on all this."

"That is nice," Cherie said warmly. "She still cares."

Miranda looked on with an approving smile. Then she glanced over at Cherie. "Mother, have you eaten anything since you've been here?"

"I'm not sure," Cherie said. "Things have been so...hectic."

"Come on, then," Miranda said, standing. "There's a deli downstairs where we can grab a bite. Michael, will they let you have anything?"

"I'd love a cup of coffee," I said. "But you'd better check with the nurse on your way out to make sure it's okay."

"Will do," Miranda said. "Come on, Mother." Cherie was busy putting on her shoes.

"Take your time," I said. "I don't think anything is going to be happening here for a while."

Cherie walked over to the bed and kissed me lightly on the lips. "*Je serai de retour, mon amour,*" she said softly. I didn't understand the words, but I got the message.

Just a few minutes after they left, my phone rang. It was Lauren.

"Hey Dad." she said. "So, it looks like I'm stranded here at Heathrow for a while. First, there was a mechanical problem with our plane, now there's a weather delay. They're saying we won't get out of here until later tonight."

"That's okay, Lauren, I'm not going anywhere. It *is* one of the busiest airports in the world. Delays are just part of the deal."

"I know, but I'm anxious to get there. Anything new?"

"Nothing that won't wait until you're here."

"I'm looking online at the Eurostar Chunnel train. I could take it and be there in a couple hours."

"The airline will get you here, just be patient. Listen, Lauren, there's something I need to tell you about. There's this family here that I've gotten to know. In fact, I've been staying with them. I met the daughter, Miranda, in Bonn and she invited me to come to Paris with them. She's about your age, you'll like her."

"That's great. I look forward to meeting her."

"Well, there's more." How do you explain this to your daughter? "Her, uh, her mother and I have become great friends. Well, we're close. I mean, don't be surprised to see us be affectionate."

"Oh my god," she said, laughing. "You've got a girlfriend!"

"No, not, well, it might not be that. Well, I guess you could say that. I'm sorry, I hope it doesn't upset you."

"No, not at all, Dad, that's cool. It's about time you got on with things, started enjoying your life." I could hear her chuckling to herself.

"Well, then," I said. "I'm looking forward to seeing you."

"I'll be there straight from the airport. Bye." I could still hear her chuckling as she hung up.

Okay, that had gone well, hadn't it?

Cherie came back from the deli, saying Miranda had gone off to run some errands for both of them. She had a paperback book she had purchased from the hospital gift store in one hand, and a large coffee for me in the other. "The nurse said coffee is on your 'approved' list," she said, handing me the cup. She looked at me carefully, like she was checking for something, and smiled. My private nurse.

I was tired, and I wasn't sure if it was the anesthesia, the new medication regimen, a lousy night of sleep, boredom, just being confined to a bed, or the effort of trying to process my condition. Probably a combination of all of them. I dozed most of the morning and into the afternoon, while Cherie read her book. Other than regular check-ins from the nursing staff, it was peaceful. Miranda returned at some point. I dozed on.

Until Cherie's voice cut into my light sleep. It said: "Michael, you have a visitor."

I opened my eyes to see Chief Malboeuf standing at the foot of my bed. For a moment, I thought it might be a bad dream, but it wasn't.

"Monsieur McCann," he said. He made a movement that was probably going to be an effort to shake my hand, but he saw all the wires and tubes and the sling, and thought better of it. "I'm very sorry that you are under the weather."

"Likewise," I said, eyeing him warily. What could he possibly want?

He must have read my thoughts. Or maybe it was the expression on my face. "I, um, I wanted to check up on you. I hope that your injuries and these other problems are resolving themselves satisfactorily." I just looked at him. "And I wanted to thank you for your assistance with our investigation, it was most beneficial." Beneficial for them, sure. Not so much for me. "I, er, we have been able to bring most of the aspects of this very unfortunate situation to a resolution. That can't of course, offset the loss of life, and the damage done to our city, our country." He sounded like a press release. "I also want you to know," at this point he glanced at Cherie, "that Detective Wolfert will be receiving a commendation for his part in the investigation. We have no corresponding acknowledgement for civilian participation, but you have our sincerest gratitude." At this point, he overcame his trepidation and stepped forward, offering his hand. I shook it. His other hand produced my passport, which he placed on the bed next to my leg. "We will be retaining your driving license, as evidence,

I'm afraid. It would appear that the attackers intentionally planted it at the scene to cast suspicion in the direction of the involvement of a U.S. citizen." No shit, Sherlock. And you fell for it. "I will wish you good day, then." With that, he spun on his heel and left the room.

I looked at Cherie. She shrugged her shoulders. "What the hell was that?" I asked. "Was that an apology? Or was that: 'let's cover our ass and make sure the American lawyer doesn't want to sue us'? Or was it as close as I'll get to a medal?"

Cherie's response was to shrug again. "Stupid policemen," was all she had to say on the matter. She sat down in her chair and went back to her book. Miranda sat in the corner, reading a newspaper, completely disinterested. It seemed like this was all just business as usual for them as the family of a cop. Not for me, but I had neither the desire nor the energy to obsess over it right then. I went back to sleep.

My first meal in the hospital arrived not much later. I had been on a "no food" restriction the night before, and for breakfast, due to my early a.m. procedure, and who knows what happened to lunch? Maybe I had been asleep. Dinner, however, arrived and was quite a disappointment. I know, hospital food isn't supposed to be great, but I was in Paris, home to some of the finest cuisine in the world. You'd think they could at least achieve something above average, but this was, for lack of a fancy French description, just plain bad. I shoved it aside and asked Miranda to bring me something from the deli. She was more than happy to have something to do.

FORTY-FOUR

Miranda woke me unintentionally, insisting in an emphatic whisper that Cherie needed to go home for a while. "Nothing's going to change, Mother," she said. "You need to go home, get some actual sleep, and change those god-awful clothes. You stink."

"I agree," I said, raising myself up in the bed. "Not about the 'stink' part, but the going home. Cherie, you need to do that. Miranda's right."

They both looked at me like I was an unexpected interloper. "Sorry we woke you," Cherie said.

"It's fine," I said. "I've done nothing but sleep all day. And I repeat: Miranda's right, you should go home and recharge. Nothing is going to happen here. And Lauren will be here sometime this evening."

"How about this, Mother?" Miranda said. "I'll go home with you, get you settled, and then I'll come back and stay with Michael until his daughter arrives." She looked at me for support.

"Sounds like an excellent plan," I said.

"Oh, all right," Cherie said, rising from the chair and stretching. "A night in a proper bed does sound good. But you call me with any news." She pointed her finger at Miranda, then me. We both nodded. "Okay, help me gather up my stuff here." Miranda started putting things into a shopping bag.

Cherie stepped over to my bed. "And you, mister, you must behave while I'm gone." Her tone softened slightly. "I really wanted to be here when your daughter arrived."

"You'll be back in the morning. You'll meet her then."

"Okay," she said, kissing me on the forehead. "If you discover you need something, let us know."

"Will do. And Cherie, thanks."

"You know my position on that."

"Yes, I do."

They exited the room, waving to me and talking to each other. I rolled over and slept some more.

An hour later Lauren blew into the room in a way that only Lauren can. She had three nurses trailing behind her, speaking French at her in a manner that told me she had pushed her way through their efforts to assist or direct her. She was carrying a huge coat, a backpack, several shopping bags, and was dragging the largest wheeled bag that the airlines would allow as a carry-on behind her. There were various items of clothing hanging out of several of the half-zipped compartments of the bag, and it made a disturbing noise that sounded like one of the wheels was about to give out.

"Dad," she said breathlessly as I turned over to face the direction of her and her entourage, "tell them who I am, that I'm supposed to be here."

I chuckled and shook my head, smiling at her. "Hello, Lauren. Nice to see you. Quite an entrance."

"Dad, please."

"*Merci beaucoup,*" I said to the cadre of nurses. "*Elle est ma...*" I searched my limited French for the word, "*ma fille*? It's O.K. My daughter." I pointed at Lauren.

The nurses relented and smiled, speaking to me in French that I couldn't begin to keep up with.

"*Merci beaucoup,*" I said again, as they began to filter out of the room. I had learned the extensive value of that small phrase in my brief time as a visitor.

"Dad," Lauren said, rushing over to the bed, "what in God's name is going on with you?" She gave me a clumsy hug through the stuff she was carrying and all the apparatus attached to my body. She pulled away, brushing against my cheek, and looked at me. She shoved her hand roughly against the side of my jaw. "What's this? Are you growing a beard?"

With Lauren, it's always hard to tell whether her attitude is one of overwhelming approval or disdain. Either way, it's intense.

"Just a little too busy to take care of that," I said.

She sat on the arm of the recliner, perched right next to my shoulder, and dropped all her stuff into a pile on the floor around her. "Okay," she said, "tell me all about it."

I proceeded to give her the *Reader's Digest* version of Dr. Patek's lengthy explanations of my heart condition. She asked intelligent questions at several junctures, and I answered them to the best of my ability. We got all the way through to my present condition, including the reason why I had to excuse myself to use the bathroom twice during the explanation.

"So, what is the deal with your head and your arm?" she asked when we were pretty much up to speed.

"Oh that," I said. "I fell."

"You fell? You mean, like when all this happened? Did you have a heart attack?"

"No, no. The Dr. has been very clear about the fact that I didn't have a heart attack. I may have been a little dizzy, or lightheaded when I fell, and that may have been related to my heart." I wasn't sure how long I could dance around this topic if she kept pushing it.

But she let me off the hook, switching gears to a subject that interested her more. "Alright," she said, grinning, "tell me about this girlfriend."

"First of all, I'm not sure whether that's the right word to use, and please don't use it in addressing her. We're friends, but we just met this week, and really haven't spent all that much time together."

She just sat there smiling at me. "Okay, Dad," she said, "spill it."

And so, I did. At least in the way you spill such things to your adult child. I took her through the history with Miranda and Paul in Bonn, coming to Paris and ending up at Cherie's house. I filled in the part about being pickpocketed, anything to avoid the other events of the last few days. I knew I would have to tell her eventually; I just wasn't ready right then. Once again, she made a good audience, asking for clarification and explanations a few times, following the story with interest.

"You'll get to meet Miranda tonight," I said in conclusion. "She'll be back up here a little later. She was actually going to stay with me until you got here, but you arrived before we expected you to."

"Oh, yeah, about that," she said. "You're also going to be paying for a Eurostar fare from London to Paris. I just couldn't wait on the airline to get their shit together." Why didn't that surprise me? "And that cab from Gare du Nord, or whatever it's called, was unbelievable! Twenty Euros? I was barely in the friggin' taxi ten minutes!"

I sighed. The truth was, I didn't care about the expense. I was just glad she was there. "That's fine, Peanut," I said. "But I'll tell you what. I'm a little worn out right now, and could really use some rest. Do you mind if I just take a small snooze? I'm told that chair you're sitting on is pretty comfortable, if you want to rest as well."

"I understand, Dad. I'm sort of jet-lagged anyway. You just rest to your heart's desire," she beamed at me. "Get it? I'll settle in here and catch some winks myself. You want this light off?"

"Sure," I said drowsily. "We'll talk more later." She clicked off the light, and I was out before she settled into the chair.

I stirred from my slumber when Miranda entered the room, but I stayed in that foggy half-sleep state, listening to the conversation between the two girls. I sensed Lauren rising from the chair and crossing the room. Both of them talked in hushed tones, in an effort not to wake me, I assumed.

"I'm Lauren," she said, "Michael's daughter."

"I'm Miranda. I'm so glad I got to meet you. I have to go back to school tomorrow, and I was afraid I would miss you."

"Likewise, for me," Lauren said. "I take it there may be some stuff between our parents that you can catch me up on."

"I don't know about that," Miranda replied. "They've been pretty close-mouthed about things. But they are obviously 'an item', at least from what I've seen."

"Well, you know more than I do. My dad never tells us kids anything. The first I heard of you, or any of this, was when he *texted* to tell me he was in the hospital. Talk about being the last to know."

"Yeah, well this whole thing has happened pretty fast. I first met your dad last week. He met my mom just this last Sunday. This whole crazy thing with the police and the Terrorism Brigade has just been the last few days..."

"Wait a minute," Lauren interrupted, "police and terrorists, what?"

"Oh," Miranda said sheepishly. "I guess I need to fill you in on that, too."

"Yes, definitely," Lauren said emphatically. "I'm just glad you and your mother have been here for him, it was hard to imagine him here in the hospital so far away, without anyone."

"My mother has been here with him since the moment they came in to the ER. I finally had to boot her out of here tonight, make her go home and get some rest. And *your* mother has been checking in with him, at least via email." There was an uncomfortable silence that followed.

"*My* mother?" asked Lauren, clearly confused.

"Oh, yes. She's emailed several times since he's been in the hospital."

More silence as Lauren pondered the facts. "I don't know who that may have been," she said hesitantly, "but it wasn't my mother. She died over four years ago."

"Oh, I'm so sorry," Miranda said in a rush, "I must be

mistaken." More confused silence. "I'm sorry, I'm sure I don't know what I'm talking about."

"Um, okay," Lauren said hesitantly. "Look, it sounds like we have a lot to discuss. Is there a restaurant or something in the hospital where we can go?"

"Sure, there's a 24-hour deli downstairs. Food's not bad."

Oh no, this did not bode well. These two could be dangerous together. I kept my eyes closed, pretending I was asleep. They left the room, talking to each other in whispers.

I used to think that life was like a train. I've more recently come to realize that it's more like a bulldozer. Big and powerful, it plows ahead, slow and steady, leveling everything in its path, a great equalizer. We just pick up the messy pieces of stuff it leaves behind, trying to do the best we can with what remains. Sometimes it works out, and there are bits of detritus than we can form into the valuable gems of our lives. Other times we're left with nothing but crap, and we do the best we can with that as well. But, regardless of our meager successes or failures, the 'dozer just keeps moving forward. Chug-chug-chug.

FORTY-FIVE

I am lying in a hospital bed in Hôpital Bichat Claude-Bernard, in Paris, France. Evening has settled in, and the room is dark except for the dim light generated by the monitor panel on a pole next to my bed, where there are several sets of numbers and wavy graphs glowing faintly over my shoulder, generated by leads attached to sticky tabs on my chest, back and abdomen. I hear a muted chime, the sound of my phone signaling the arrival of an email message. I reach over to the tray by the bed and pull the phone loose from its charger, resting it in my left hand atop the sheets covering my lap. The screen bathes the upper part of my body and the bed in a bubble of blueish light. With my right index finger, I poke the email icon, and the message appears on the screen. The content is concise: "You've had your fun, Mick. Time to come home."

I squint my eyes at the screen and read it again, just to be sure:

"You've had your fun, Mick. Time to come home."

Part Two

Living in Paris

FORTY-SIX

The doctor should have been at home, resting comfortably in his bed next to his wife, his two children slumbering in adjacent rooms. Instead, he was at the hospital, reviewing charts in preparation for morning rounds. It was well after the dinner hour, but he had not yet eaten, and his stomach growled in protest at the deprivation. As he reviewed the charts, a series of alarms sounded from the nearby nurse's station.

"What is it?" he asked, looking up at the nurse on duty.

"It's room 17, he's coding," she replied, with a hint of panic in her voice.

"Grab the cart," the doctor said, quickly rising from his chair. "Meet me there." He took off at a measured run toward room 17.

In the room, the doctor found the patient unconscious on his back in the bed, hands limp across his abdomen, head rolled to one side, a cell phone resting on his motionless chest. The monitor on a pole next to the bed was emitting a shrill squeal, its lights flashing. The doctor listened with his stethoscope while feeling for a pulse in the man's neck. He moved the stethoscope a few inches to the right and listened for another second. As he did so, the nurse entered the room pushing a mobile defibrillation cart, followed by another nurse and an orderly. She pushed the cart up next to the bed, at the doctor's left hip.

"No pulse," he said, tossing the stethoscope around his neck. "Prep him for defib."

The second nurse rushed to the far side of the bed, removing the phone and yanking at the front of the patient's hospital gown, tearing the ties loose and pulling it from his torso, baring his chest. The doctor simultaneously grabbed the handles on the backs of two metal paddles from the cart and held them out as the other nurse dabbed their surfaces with gel from a tube. He rubbed the paddles together and placed them on the patient's chest. He shoved the coiled wires that connected the paddles to the cart aside with his elbow.

"All clear," he said firmly. After a moment's hesitation, he pulled the trigger on the handle of the right paddle and the patient's body jumped upward, the chest rising. The doctor handed the paddles back to the nurse, whipped his stethoscope into place and again listened to the patient. "Still no pulse," he said, returning the stethoscope to his neck. "Again." He reached back and to the side, and the nurse thrust the paddles into his hands. He rubbed them together again and placed them back on the patient's chest. "All clear."

The events repeated, except this time the doctor listened longer through the stethoscope, adjusting its location several times. "Sinus rhythm?" he asked, glancing up toward the monitor. The second nurse punched some buttons on the monitor and stared at it for a second. The alarm stopped squealing and the lights stopped flashing. A ragged line of green light bounced across the darkened screen.

"Sinus rhythm," she responded in a relieved tone.

"Well done, then," the doctor said as the nurse placed the paddles back onto the cart. "Thank you, everyone."

Nearly two hours later, the doctor trudged out of the service entrance at the rear of the hospital. Tired. Bone-weary. And still hungry. He hoisted the strap of his leather duffle over his shoulder, freeing his right hand to dig for the car keys in his trousers pocket, careful not to spill the coffee he carried in his other hand. He pulled the keys out, angling across the asphalt parking area toward his reserved spot. He stopped short as he saw the space before him occupied by a red sports car that was not his. He grumbled to himself as he recalled that the car had been parked in his space when he arrived earlier in the day, forcing him to find a spot on the far side of the lot.

"God damn it," he said out loud as he stepped up to the side of the car. "Still here." He looked at the rich interior of the car, its top down, the buttery tan leather almost glowing under the overhead security lights. He glanced around furtively, and then emptied the contents of the coffee cup onto the driver's seat.

"Probably a fucking plastic surgeon," he muttered as he walked away.

FORTY-SEVEN

"We will be placing a device just like this one in a small pocket we will create under the flesh, just about here." Dr. Patek touched me lightly on the left side of my chest, an inch or two below my collarbone, as he held a small object in front of me with his other hand. It had a smooth surface with the appearance of stainless steel, rounded edges, and looked like a tiny cell phone. "We will run leads from this through the blood vessels into your heart," he went on, "where they will monitor your cardiac activity and pace your heartbeat, as necessary. Additionally, the device will provide an electrical shock to defibrillate your heart if it should go into an abnormal pattern for any length of time, or if it should stop beating altogether."

I was sitting on the exam table in his clinical office suite on the lower level of Hôpital Bichat Claude-Bernard, shirt off, while he was explaining to me in very calm tones that they would be cutting me open, implanting this foreign object into my chest, while stopping my heart so that they could insert and secure wires into my heart muscle, all in an effort to keep me alive and kicking. Well, at least alive. At that point in time, I hadn't felt much like kicking anything. I was doing well just to walk across the room. This contraption was supposed to fix that. Well, maybe not fix, but at least help.

I had been in the hospital for about a week following my diagnosis of congestive heart failure and the frightening events that followed. Things had not improved much in the interim, and Dr. Patek had decided that I needed the implantation of a pacemaker/defibrillator to keep me pumping correctly and prevent a repeat performance.

I nodded my understanding, slightly daunted by the procedures being presented. Especially the part about stopping my heart. I thought that the whole idea was to prevent that from happening. Again.

With medical professionals, you pretty much have to take them on faith. Sure, you can get second, third or fourth opinions, but in the end, you simply have to trust the one you select, and that they know what they're doing. I had that kind of trust in Dr. Patek. He had, after all, saved my life once already.

"Okay," I said, still digesting it all. "When do we do this thing?"

"Tomorrow, I think," he replied. "We'll get you prepared tonight, and then the surgical team will come for you early in the morning." His British accent made it all sound so pleasant and reasonable. "You'll be here another day or two for recovery and monitoring. You'll be home by week's end." Pleasant and reasonable. Stopping my heart.

"Sounds good," I said with false enthusiasm. "Let's get on with it."

The surgery went without a hitch. I awoke with a fuzzy head and only a little pain at the incision site. Cherie was reading a book in the chair at my bedside. This scene was becoming too familiar.

"Hey," I said, rolling my head toward her.

"You are awake!" She said, standing and putting the book aside. "How do you feel?"

"Not bad. Better than I expected."

"The doctor says you will be able to go home tomorrow."

"Good, I'm sick of this place." I tried to chuckle. It hurt a little.

"I can take care of you at home just as well as they can here."

"No doubt in my mind." I smiled wanly at her and she

stroked my forehead affectionately. I drifted off back into anesthesia world.

And so I had become the International Bionic Man: an American who, by way of a surgery performed in France by a physician from India, had been implanted with a medical device designed in Sweden, assembled and sold by a Canadian company, using components manufactured in South Korea and several other spots around the globe. I could almost see Lee Majors flying across the screen and hear the basso profundo voice-over in the background: *"We have the technology."*

Not that I was ready to leap any tall buildings. I was beginning to come to terms with the limitations I would be facing. There is a unique kind of disappointment you feel when your own body lets you down. You rely on it your entire life, taking for granted that it will just keep chugging along, requiring only general maintenance and occasional minor repairs. But then it breaks down on you, leaving you stranded by the side of the road. It gets your attention. And makes you appreciate the medical mechanics that can get you up and running, back to normal. Or as near to normal as possible.

FORTY-EIGHT

I wasn't a reluctant Parisian, at least I hadn't come to think of myself in that way during the months since my cardiac crisis. Living in Paris long-term simply hadn't been the plan, more the result of serendipity. Much like my original foray into the city, and I just stayed on as if I were unable to leave. Perhaps that was a truth I was hesitant to acknowledge.

I considered myself lucky to have found a cardiologist I trusted with my life. I had been put in touch with an excellent therapist who seemed to understand my American angst, and I was in a relationship with a woman who was as close to the personification of perfection as I could ever hope to deserve. And I didn't really want to go home.

Home was a law practice that was slogging along on autopilot, home was my kids and grandchildren, along with the duties and responsibilities that accompany them, and home was a place that seemed to have chased me away and hidden itself in obscurity. Home seemed to have lost all the allure and comfort of, well, home.

Paris was another place altogether. It was a place where I had begun to feel a level of contentment which had been evading me for a long time. It was the antithesis of "home". Paris was "away". "Away" felt good at that point.

Being "away" hadn't stopped my life from moving forward. Cherie and I had been looking at new housing in the challenging Paris market. She was in the process of selling her family home and we were looking for an upscale flat to replace it; a downsize in space and a release from the drudgery of home maintenance for her. A place where we would live together. Yet another new experience for me.

"I can't wait to be rid of that albatross," she told me when I asked if she would find it difficult to sell the home where she had grown up and raised her own children. "I am ready for something less than four levels, fewer than three bathrooms, with no garden, no aging roof and no weathered paint to maintain." She was, in short, more than ready to bid her historical Parisian row house *adieu*.

"This is Michael, my fiancé," she said when introducing me to Edgard, our real estate broker. This despite the fact that she was fully aware that we were not getting married. She was fine with that fact, but refused to refer to me as her "boyfriend".

"Boyfriends are for schoolgirls and gay men," she had espoused firmly. "I am neither."

It was a perfect time to look at property in Paris. It was actually a perfect time to do anything in Paris, at least in my opinion; mid-October, just a month past the autumnal equinox, well into the cooler, grayer days of Paris' year. Springtime in Paris may be what the balladeers croon about, but autumn in Paris beats springtime hands down, as far as I'm concerned. Forget the flowers, the birds, the sunshine. The fall season of transition seemed to suit my contemplative, melancholy personality to a tee. I understand that it's not for everyone. But in one of the most visited cities in Europe, the off-season results in a dramatic drop in the tourist presence that is very noticeable. Museums and the historic attractions are less crowded. The bars, restaurants and public areas are uncongested, and the Metro is packed and hectic only during rush hours.

We were meeting Edgard outside a two-bedroom flat in the 3rd Arrondissement, near the Marais district. He was late, as seemed to be the norm for him, and we were sitting on a bench across the street from the building where the flat was located. The air had a bit of nip in it, but it wasn't really cold, and the sky was a pleasant, overcast hue of blue-gray that I found to be soothing.

Cherie took my hand in hers, rubbing her thumb across my palm. "Did you take your medicines?" she asked. Ever the vigilant nurse.

"I did," I responded, giving her hand a squeeze. My drug regimen was something to which I had theretofore been unaccustomed, and I needed all the help I could get in remembering to take the six pills a day I had been prescribed. And I had noticed that I could feel a difference if I missed a dosage or got the timing out of whack, a fact that caused me more than minor consternation. I was not used to being kept physically in line by way of drug therapy. But there I was.

"Oh, there's Edgard!" Cherie said, jumping up from the bench. She waved to get his attention, and he crossed the street in our direction.

"*Bon après-midi,*" he said as he approached, shaking both our hands. Cherie immediately launched into a French conversation with him, and knowing that he spoke very little English, I wasn't really listening while tagging along as we crossed the street and entered the building. Edgard worked a series of locks and codes to gain access to the foyer, and we walked up to the third floor, which in France is actually the fourth floor, the first being referred to as the "ground" floor. I noticed that Cherie kept sneaking glances at me as we ascended, and I have to admit that I was a little winded by the time we had made four rotations of the circular stairway, but I tried to keep it to myself.

"Edgard says there is a lift," Cherie told me quietly as Edgard was fiddling with the lock on the door into the flat. "It's at the rear entrance, where you come in from the parking."

"Not a problem," I said, feeling like a complete invalid. It was something I'd wrestled with since my initial diagnosis. I had never experienced any major health issues before, so having to plan an outing around how many stairs were involved or how far it was between Metro stops was something that I found extremely frustrating. I tried to do the best I could, and hide the effects. Suck it up.

The flat was impressive, though not to my personal taste. Very modern, very European, lots of chrome and glass and minimalist decor. None of the traditional French Provincial that the exterior architecture of the building promised. I knew Cherie would be ambivalent about it. She was. She pointed out to Edgard that this property wasn't actually in the Marais district, but merely on the fringes. He apologized, and said he would limit future possibilities to within the boundaries of the district. All this according to the translation Cherie provided after the fact.

Montmartre had been my initial experience with the city, my first love, so to speak. It would appear that Les Marais was to become my adult experience; more textured, more nuanced, more slowly appreciated. I was ready, I was not holding back at all. I just needed to immerse myself gradually, to feel the waters and adjust to the currents as I made my way across the submerged terrain. Cherie was not really about wading carefully into currents, her style was more akin to diving in, head first, with no concern for what might lie in the depths. It was much of what I loved about her.

Les Marais is to Montmartre what a sophisticated older sister is to a teenage girl; wiser, more worldly, more polished and, perhaps most importantly, more mature in her beauty. The Marais district was originally home to the noble class, based on proximity to the Palace of Versailles, and the buildings and common areas reflect that gentrified air, despite the fact that the district has fallen into disrepair at several junctures in its history.

After my release from the hospital following my heart issues, I stayed at Cherie's for several weeks, convalescing and enjoying the benefits of personal nursing. As soon as I was back on my feet, though, I felt the need to assert my independence, and, much to Cherie's disappointment, I found myself a small studio apartment on Rue Gabrielle, in Montmartre. It was barely adequate for an American, everything from bedroom to kitchen to living area crammed into a single 12-by-18-foot room. The tiny bathroom was an afterthought, a tiled stall containing toilet, sink and shower, with a half-size hot water heater mounted up against the ceiling in a corner over the toilet. You could pee, brush your teeth and wash your hair simultaneously. And no air conditioning, which is the case in much of Paris, where it can get quite warm in the summer. That particular summer it did, and I found myself missing the luxury of American central air conditioning on many occasions during the months of June and July. I purchased three different types of fans from Monoprix, and stationed them around the room so as to maximize the air flow, especially in the corner where the bed was located.

Despite the warm summer months, I had been enjoying my residence on Rue Gabrielle, not far from the hostel where I had stayed upon my initial arrival. It was my authentic introduction to life in Paris, the first few months of a completely new chapter in my life, and I wouldn't have changed any of it.

Just around the corner from my apartment was a traditional Parisian grocery, with a broad burgundy awning, wooden produce stands out front, and haphazard, rickety wooden shelving inside, called Au Marché de la Butte. In a bin out front were rolled-up posters for sale, a splashy montage of images promoting a movie called *Amelie*. I realized at once that this was the same film I had first encountered back at Café des Deux Moulins during my early days in Paris, and asked Cherie about it one day while we were at the store. She laughed, saying: "Oh, it is this shop's claim to fame! It's a funny, quirky little film starring Audrey Tautou, and this market is featured prominently in the story, but it's called Maison Collignon. We shall have to rent it sometime; you will be quite amused." And so we did, and so I was. And I bought the poster.

Now we were looking at places a few socio-economic steps up from my little Montmartre studio. They all had central air. They all had modern kitchens, balconies with great urban views, and spacious, high-ceilinged rooms. And all of them were at a price point in the several-hundred-thousand Euros. Cherie didn't flinch at the prices, she had, after all, listed her house at twice the amount of the price tags on the places we were looking at, and the expectation was that she would easily get her asking price. She would, however, hear nothing of any financial participation on my part. I didn't want to fight that theoretical battle at that point, we could sort all of it out when, and if, our plans became reality.

FORTY-NINE

I am eating a box lunch on a wooden bench in the Jardins des Champs-Élysées, at the far end of the commercial part of the boulevard from the Arche de Triomphe. It is a cool, sunny day and there are hordes of people, tourists and natives, milling up and down the corridor that shoots northwest from the Place de la Concorde.

There are gray pigeons at my feet, glancing up at me expectantly, hoping for a breadcrumb or some bird seed. They will be disappointed.

I have been out of the hospital for about a month following my device implantation surgery, and I am on one of the many sojourns I have been making to test my legs, endurance and, ultimately, my heart. But this particular afternoon I am not musing about my cardiac stamina. I am wondering if Cherie truly understands how locked away my emotions are, what a big hill she has to climb to reach me. She seems inexhaustible in her willingness to try. I find myself admiring her for the effort.

A man in a tan trench coat walks by with a small dog on a leash, gravel crunching beneath his shoes. The pigeons scatter just long enough to let the dog pass, then return to harass me. I continue to eat my sandwich, trying to ignore them, but I can't help it, I find myself staring at them.

I am fascinated by their bizarre eyes; bright red rims, strange opaque pastel-colored irises. They cock their small heads to look at me, pleading with me, one eye at a time. As I *puzzle over this odd behavior, I stare back at them and realize that, with their eyes mounted so far on the sides of their skulls, they can view me clearly only by looking at me obliquely, that they can't see me at all if they look at me head-on.*

FIFTY

It's not as simple as you might think to walk out of one life and into another. After I made the decision to stay in Paris, I was confronted with a few realities that needed to be taken care of. The first, and toughest, was the decision to put my house in Portland on the market. There wasn't necessarily a sentimental attachment for me; it hadn't been our family homestead, my kids weren't raised there, but Patty and I had moved there after the kids were all out of the nest, and it had been our home during the last few years of her life. Parting with it was like surrendering the last vestiges of a period in my life which had been both indelible and bittersweet. It was probably time. The fiscal reality was that we'd paid cash for it, the Portland real estate market had exploded in the last few years, and I was going to need the highly inflated price it would bring, so onto the market it went.

The second challenge was dealing with my law practice. I had made arrangements for a young attorney to cover my contractual responsibilities with the Juvenile Court during what I had initially planned as an absence of a month or two. He'd kept at it after that time had passed, and had proven to be fairly adept at handling my other clients as well.

"He gets it," my legal assistant Meredith told me during one of our long-distance conferences. "He approaches clients and cases the same way you do," she went on. "He's interested in their problems, and solving them, before the money meter clicks in. Clients are aware of that."

Ultimately, he had simply taken over my contract with the

Multnomah County Court, and we were operating the rest of my practice on a shared fee/expense arrangement that seemed to be working fairly well. The one thing I had made absolutely clear to everyone involved was that Meredith would be taken care of, no matter what.

Another necessity was dealing with my legal status in France. You can stay in France on an American passport, as a tourist, for up to 90 days. A longer stay requires a visa. However, you have to obtain that visa before coming to France, which created a classic Catch-22 situation for me. I was in the process of getting my long-term status approved based on my ongoing medical care, and after multiple filings through the American consulate with letters and records submitted by my doctor, I appeared to be getting close. Most people probably would have thrown up their hands in frustration, given up and gone home. Sometimes being a lawyer, and being accustomed to dealing with all the bureaucratic bullshit, has its advantages.

That applied to my health insurance issues as well. Suffice it to say that my U.S. insurance company, who shall remain nameless, did not want to cover any of my medical bills incurred in a foreign country, due to the fact that the facilities and doctors were "out of network", until I reminded them that I had inquired about such coverage before leaving on my trip, and that they had assured me that I would be covered. And, yes, that conversation had been recorded by their own convenient telecommunications system. Big Brother can be a good thing under certain circumstances.

Then there was the matter of continuing coverage for my extended stay. After my agreement to pay an outlandishly expensive premium, I had health coverage for at least one additional year. Maybe by then, depending on my visa status, I could qualify for the French national plan. Not that they would be thrilled about signing up an over-the-hill expat with a heart condition. Or maybe they wouldn't care, the French seemed to be very laid back about that kind of thing.

Cherie, at several junctures, pointed out that if we were to get married it would resolve most of the problems quite easily. She had, much to my surprise, quietly processed the necessary paperwork to transform her long-standing separation from Gregor into a legal divorce over the summer months. The only way I found out was when I raised it as an impediment to one of her proposals. The marriage suggestion was always met on my part with appreciation and seriousness, but it never seemed like the right solution to me.

My new therapist in Paris was Dr. Isadore Guiome. She looked a little like Barbara Bush. A younger version, but with the same stately demeanor and a head full of well-coiffed white hair. She also shared the innate charm and mischievous twinkle in her eye. I was hooked minutes into our first session, even though she was not exactly fluent in English. You would think that such would be a disadvantage in therapy, but we discovered that the need to be precise in order to overcome the language challenges helped to broaden the scope of our sessions, at the same time making them more intimate. We actually forayed into some areas which had been difficult for me to fully explore with Bob. Like Patty's death. What most people perceived at the time as her sudden death.

It had been anything but sudden for me. Patty had been insistent about keeping her diagnosis to ourselves, not even sharing it with the kids. "They have lives to live, things to do besides worry about me," she had said. "And there's nothing they can do, anyway." We argued at the time, with me saying it was a selfish attitude on her part, and her insisting that it was best for everyone. As was usual, it really didn't matter who was right or wrong, her will won out.

Brain cancer, especially as progressed as hers was, can be brutal in its onslaught and almost merciful in the rapidity of progression. Within a month of her initial diagnosis she began battling symptoms, within several more she was struggling to maintain normalcy everywhere but at home, and just after the agonizing sixth-month anniversary of that fateful visit to her doctor she succumbed.

I woke up to find her comatose after having a long conversation with her just the night before. She had been at work just two days prior, coming home from the office on that Friday afternoon saying she didn't feel "quite one-hundred percent." By Sunday morning, with Patty unable to participate, I had to break the news to the kids. In less than a week she was gone.

The quick, natural exit had been her choice. "Inoperable" is how they described her condition, but they presented several "Hail Mary" options for treatment and palliative care.

"No," she'd said, stopping the conversation in its tracks, "I will die privately and gracefully, not drugged-out, being assaulted by an army of doctors." In the end, as was so typical of her life, she'd had her way. I was left to pick up the pieces.

I spent a long time resenting her for leaving me to deal with the kids alone. And then I struggled mightily with the guilt I felt over being royally pissed off at her, and then the remorse I would experience over the way my guilt and anger began to color the only part of her that I had left: her memory. And I would desperately miss her calming, sound advice which always grounded me during the most difficult times, which those undoubtedly were. It was a no-win situation. It sucked.

To my relief, Dr. Guiome and I had been able to move forward on some issues that I'd never made much headway with while working with Bob, who seemed to be fixated on the concept of "closure". It occurred to me that it might be because Dr. Guiome was a woman. Maybe I was willing to be more forthcoming and vulnerable with her, willing to go to some of the more difficult places. Or maybe she wasn't so preoccupied with "closure". Perhaps there wasn't a French word for it.

Someone gave me a copy of Joan Didion's *The Year of Magical Thinking* not long after Patty's death. I'm sure they thought it would help. It did not. I was not able, or ready, to examine the raw wound that was my grief in the way Didion did very publicly in her book. I lacked the bravery to do it in that fashion. I was existing at the time in a perpetually altered state, high on continuous doses of denial. I'm unsure as to whether Joan Didion would have approved. Bob did not.

Dr. Guiome, on the other hand, did not seem to find any of it unhealthy or unresolved. She just nodded and understood. Perhaps it was the difference between European and American psychotherapy. My money was on the Europeans, they'd been at it a lot longer than we Yanks. Or maybe, once again, it could be attributed to the language barrier.

Inevitably, the topic of my "phantom" emails from my then-deceased wife during the prior year came up in my sessions. Dr. Guiome seemed unphased by it. She gently pushed it back at me, asking me what I thought the communications meant or represented. No judgement, no dismissal, no confronting me with the absurdity. She allowed me to take ownership of what had been my truth, make of it whatever I felt to be significant, or not.

The emails were also the subject of several weighty conversations with Cherie. Surprisingly, she didn't belabor the issue after figuring out what had been going on. Or not going on. The circumstances surrounding that revelation were tumultuous, but when the dust eventually settled, she was content to sit back and patiently wait for me to bring it up. Her eventual response initially surprised me, but upon reflection I realized how consistent it was with her personality, with the person she was.

"Michael, these are not things that we are wise enough to fully understand," she said calmly. "Does it really matter what has happened in your journey to reconstruct your life? I am not here to pass judgement on what might be imagined or real, what is therapeutic or crazy. I am here only to love you and to accept what is your reality as a part of mine."

I was amazed at her practical, open-minded attitude

toward an issue that could have been loaded with emotion and prejudice. Her message was simple: "Let yourself off the hook."

"And," she continued, in our final conversation on the matter, "can you truly say that this was not real? Can you tell me that, beyond the shadow of a doubt, these things did not occur? I cannot. There are things that none of us can know. Who are we to say that we understand everything in this complicated world?"

It made me wonder if she and Dr. Guiome had been in cahoots, conspiring to keep my sanity intact, both of them gently embracing my experience rather than using it as a bludgeon to knock me back into the real world. I was simply thankful that they were both able to be unconditionally supportive. Maybe it was a French thing, a philosophical attitude rooted in the long history of a people unfazed by whatever impossible, mysterious thing might be thrown at them. Of course, the ever-philosophical French have an expression that fits: "*Il n'est rien de réel que le rêve et l'amour*"; "Nothing is real but dreams and love."

FIFTY-ONE

*T*he digital clock on the bookshelf reads 1:30 a.m. I can
see it over the thick eiderdown comforter that covers
Cherie and me as we sprawl on her overstuffed sofa. The fire
in the hearth has died down to embers, but still emits a small
amount of heat. The television screen is snowy and silent, the
movie we had been watching long over.

Cherie is sleeping, her head against my chest. Her mouth
moves slightly as she breathes, a small puffing sound slipping between her lips with each breath. I gaze at her in the
flickering glow from the fireplace, her face bathed in the soft
light. She is lovely, not beautiful in the traditional sense, not
a Catherine Deneuve. But still a handsome French woman
with smoldering eyes, flawless skin, dense dark hair and a
soft, sensual mouth. She turns heads. I have seen it happen
as we stroll through the markets or board the Metro. People,
not just men, are drawn to her. She radiates a warmth and
serenity that causes eyes to come to rest on her, ears to tune
to her soft voice, souls to seek her presence. She is magnetic.

I wonder at what has brought us together. Perhaps I'm
the interesting anomaly thrown into her world by circumstances and fate, the wounded American in Paris in need of
an angel, an entertaining escape from an otherwise traditional life. I don't really care; I realize that I am the benefi-
ciary of a gift that far exceeds any expectation or entitlement
I could ever imagine. She is nothing short of my personal
saving grace.

I am happy, as happy as I've ever been. I enjoy our life,

Paris, the everyday ups and downs of our existence, the ebb and flow of familiarity and excitement that marks our days.

I ponder whether or not I have ever really understood the concept of love. I was married and completely committed to a woman for nearly three decades. We raised children, faced adversity, weathered difficulties, celebrated triumphs, and supported each other through it all. But I don't remember a moment where the heavens opened and revealed to me a universe of emotion labeled as "love." It was a relationship far too complex to be encompassed by a single four-letter word.

This life with Cherie is a very different thing from that.

I extract my hand carefully from under the comforter and gently stroke her hair. She stirs slightly in response, but doesn't wake up. I recall the first time I saw her standing in the doorway as she welcomed me into her home for a meal. Nothing magical, no bands playing, no fireworks erupting. Yet we have ended up here. Intertwined, literally and figuratively, in a life together. We don't have all the history of my marriage, only the here and now. And, perhaps most importantly, tomorrow. Maybe the four-letter label, with all its elusive promise, belongs here.

The clock on the bookshelf catches my eye again as it clicks over to read 1:48 a.m. I squeeze my arm around Cherie's shoulders and she raises her head.

"Time for bed, chérie," I say softly, kissing her gently on her warm cheek.

FIFTY-TWO

The apartment hunting spilled over into late Fall. Cherie's house drew several very nice offers, a couple at higher than asking price, but she opted not to accept any of them, feeling like the market would rise even more after the first of the year. I maintained the studio in Montmartre, although I actually spent very little time there. There were periods of time when we didn't seem to be in a hurry to find this flat which we would be moving into. It wasn't that either of us was dragging our feet, or that we were being overly picky. It just seemed that the right place had not come along, and we were both comfortable with that. Cherie said that it would probably be the place she would live for the rest of her life, and that she wanted it to be perfect. Edgard didn't seem to be losing patience with us, although it was a little hard for me to tell, given the language challenge.

The language difficulty, or my inability to overcome it, had become a point of contention. Cherie claimed I just wasn't trying. I claimed I wasn't good at languages. I was also stubborn; learning a new language seemed like school to me, and I'd never been very fond of school. Strange, I know, for someone with a post-graduate degree, but there you have it. I was working on it, but my approach was more functional than academic. I was learning enough to get by, to meet my everyday needs, but not much beyond that. I had no feeling of obligation to become fluent in the language simply because I was living in the country. As much as I was aware that my attitude reflected the worst of the egocentric mindset of the

"Ugly American", it was the way I felt. And the reality was that so many Parisians were at least conversant in English that it was pretty easy to get by. I guess that made me both stubborn and lazy.

Cherie and I were having lunch at a brasserie near one of the apartments we had just looked at. Edgard had been very enthused about this particular prospect, Cherie much less so. It had been so-so in my estimation, not a lot different than several others we had viewed.

We were winding our way through the brasserie's outdoor tables, looking for an empty one. A musical combo of two young men on guitar and drums, both wearing sunglasses, played quietly in the corner of the outdoor seating area.

"Michael!"

I heard the shout from over my right shoulder, and turned to see who was hailing me. Before I got turned all the way around, the wild tangle of blonde hair sparked immediate recognition.

"Ilona," I said calmly, trying to dampen her enthusiasm, or at least her volume level. I reached my hand out in her direction. She ignored the hand and nearly knocked me down with a full-body embrace.

"*Mon amour!*" she said as she shook her blonde mane, which had only grown in mass since I had last seen her, clearing her face to look up at me. I realized that she had on the same green apron as the other waitresses in the restaurant, and concluded, logically, that she worked there.

I gave her a squeeze and smiled at her impish countenance. "I thought you were going to America," I said.

"Oh, America," she said disdainfully, still clinging to me. "It is so long to go there. I don't have the time or money to waste. I started working here, and, well, here I am still!" She glanced past my shoulder and saw Cherie. "Oh, so she is why you could not be father to my baby. Very pretty. I don't blame you."

Cherie smiled pleasantly and nodded in response.

I turned, unsuccessfully attempting to pull myself from Ilona's grasp, and gestured toward Cherie. "Ilona," I said, "Cherie. Cherie, Ilona."

"So very pleased to meet you," Cherie said graciously, placing her hand lightly on Ilona's arm, which was still wrapped tightly around my torso.

"I am sorry," Ilona responded, still smiling broadly, "but I tease Michael. He was so kind to my offer; he did not break my heart. I love him still!"

Her response didn't really make much sense, and certainly didn't make things any better, so I looked around warily and asked: "Shouldn't you get back to work? I don't want to get you fired."

"I should," she said, bouncing up onto her toes, giving me a peck on the cheek. "But it is so good to see you! And to meet you, Cherie." She disentangled herself from our awkward embrace, spun around quickly and flashed a smile back over her shoulder as she departed.

After she had gone, I leaned over to Cherie and asked: "Would you like an explanation?"

"Not at all," she replied, smiling slyly. "It is not necessary." In her unflappable French manner, Cherie seemed to be completely unaffected by the encounter.

We found a table and, thankfully, Ilona was not our waitress. We actually had a waiter, who brought us water, no ice, along with menus, and waited expectantly as we looked at them. We ordered under his passive gaze and discussed the apartment situation after he exited. The combo was playing Beatles tunes. They were pretty good.

"I hope Edgard has a grasp of that intangible 'thing' I am looking for," Cherie said. "Do you understand it?"

"I think I'll know it when I see it."

Cherie looked thoughtful, sipping her water. "Maybe we should get a new realtor."

I raised my eyebrows and looked at her emphatically "Really? You want to do that to him? After all the time and effort he's put in? You know he only gets paid if you buy a place."

"I know, I know. But I am getting impatient."

I nodded. "Let's give it a few more weeks. It seems like there are new places coming on the market all the time."

"All right. You are always rational about these things. I will be patient." She reached across the table and placed her hand gently over mine.

I smiled and gazed into her hazel eyes. I couldn't deny how good it made me feel.

FIFTY-THREE

This was not destined to be a moment of triumph.

The man with the missing finger sorted through the canvas vests leaning against the wall of the dark cellar, lined up on the dirt floor. Each held six blocks of gray-colored plastic explosive in pockets hand-stitched into the inner surface of the vest. Black and red wires ran from a metal cylinder embedded in each block through the canvas to a detonator attached to the back of the vest. Another set of wires, wrapped in black electrical tape, ran from the detonator to a trigger device, tucked into a pocket on the front of each vest. Fabric packets of steel ball-bearings accompanied each gray rectangle of explosive, positioned against their exterior surfaces.

Each vest contained enough explosive to kill or cause catastrophic damage within a radius of 20 meters, and an area of serious injury beyond that. The wearer of the vest would, of course, be obliterated.

The man poked the lower edge of the vest nearest him with the toe of his boot. He swallowed hard against the bile rising in his throat as he realized that his faith had waned. His zeal no longer sustained him. His hatred still burned, but it had become more self-consuming than motivational.

No, this would not be a moment of triumph. It was a moment of desperation. His mind told him that in just a few hours it would be over. He knew in his heart that it would never really be over.

FIFTY-FOUR

I was talking to my oldest son, Peter, on the phone. He's a commercial real estate broker, and was helping me with the sale of my house.

"The buyers are asking for a 30-day extension on the closing," he said. "Something to do with their financing."

"That's okay," I said, "I can wait 30 more days."

"Alright, I'll let them know."

"How're your siblings?" I asked.

He sighed. "Well, you know Lauren, it's always brain surgery in the middle of a three-ring-circus at 100 miles an hour with her. Never a dull moment. Jeff's still a barista. Looks like that's his life plan." Peter had never been fond of Lauren's husband, Jeff.

"He's a manager now," I said neutrally.

"Oh, so now he's a barista in charge of a bunch of other baristas, I guess. Good for him." The sarcasm dripped through the international connection.

"Give him a break. He's a good father. And he puts up with your sister."

"Huh, yeah, I'll give him that." I was pretty sure he was referring to the sister part, not the father observation. "Let's see," he went on, "Rich is doing well. He's got a regular 'gig' at a recording studio called 'Nashville North'. And he's playing the coffee house/bar circuit. But the studio thing pays the bills. You should go see him next time you come home, if you fly in through New York. I saw him last summer when I was there. He's really pretty good." High praise from an older brother.

"I'll do that," I said. "How about you? How are the kids?"

"Kids are great. Colton's hockey team is in first place, going into the final stretch. Jeremy's more interested in video games than sports. Both getting good grades."

"And Kaitlyn?" His wife.

He chuckled. "She's great too. Dealing with her house full of men." Kaitlyn had grown up in a family of four sisters, no brothers. Now she had all boys to contend with, including Peter. "She's working down at the office a couple days a week. Keeps us from having to hire a secretary that we really don't need. Gets her outta the house."

"Lauren's kids?"

"You know, we don't see them that much. I guess the youngest is having some trouble at school, they think he might be dyslexic. I think he's just a lot like his mother, but nobody asked me."

"Probably should keep that to yourself, then."

"Yeah, I know. Don't hear much about the other two, I guess that means they're fine. You know what a conversation with Lauren is like: 'Hi, the world is on fire; Peace, Love and Understanding; you look like shit; gotta go skydiving or some other fuckin' thing, bye-bye'."

My turn to chuckle. "Just make sure she's okay for me. Big brother duty."

"Oh, I will. I do. Hey I got another call coming in. Take care, and try to make it home for Christmas, all the kids miss Grandpa."

"I will see what I can do. I'll definitely try. Love to all."

"Same back atcha. Bye, Dad." Click. Buzz.

Those conversations always left me in a state of confusion. I missed my kids. I was missing big parts of my grandkids' lives. I felt something like guilt over that, but not regret. Did that make me a bad parent or grandparent? I didn't feel qualified to make that judgment.

I thought about the non-committal commitment I'd just

made regarding Christmas. The holidays had been tough in recent years. Patty had died in mid-November, and it had cast a pall over the holiday season for my family ever since. This would be the fifth Christmas without her. Perhaps enough time had passed to make it easier. I didn't know. I certainly hadn't planned on being gone; my original European trip was expected to be wrapped up long before then.

My phone rang while I was still holding it, startling me. I answered without looking at the screen.

"I found it, Michael, or, rather, we found it! Edgard came through!"

It was Cherie. Her excitement was palpable, even over the phone. She had, evidently, found a flat that fit the bill.

"Great! Tell me about it."

"Oh, I can't begin to, you have to see it!"

"Alright, when can I look at it?"

"Well, it's too late tonight. But first thing in the morning. It's perfect! You are going to love it! I'll call Edgard and get it set up. Do you have anything in the morning?"

"No, I'm completely open. I have an appointment with Dr. Guiome here in," I glanced down, holding out my phone to check the time, then pressing it back to my ear, "about thirty minutes."

"Okay, I'll call Edgard and call you back."

"Okay. I can't wait."

I hung up, smiling. I really was excited for her, for us. It wasn't a moment I'd been dreading, but it was going to bring quite a few issues to the forefront, issues I'd been kicking down the road for quite a while.

I had just walked out of the Metro station closest to Dr. Guiome's office. I was in the upper part of the 20th Arrondissement, in a trendy little area with quite a few professional offices and financial firms. My appointment was at eight o'clock. Evening professional appointments are common in France, while morning appoints are nearly impossible to come by. A different sort of workday. I liked it.

The building where Dr. Guiome's office was located had a nice lobby with a seating area under a glassed-in atrium containing large plants and a koi pond. I sat among the greenery and listened to the calming burble of the water feature as I waited for my appointment time to roll around. An elderly woman in a red wool coat and matching beret sat opposite me, reading a book, her wooden cane hooked over the arm of her chair. The janitorial staff ran vacuums over the carpet on the second-floor balcony overlooking the atrium.

I smiled, still amused at Cherie's excitement over finding the perfect apartment. My guess was that it was smack in the heart of Les Marais, had two large bedrooms, at least two full bathrooms and an ample balcony overlooking a picturesque view with enough outdoor space to grow a small herb garden in containers. It would be on at least the third floor, but not above the fifth, and would have an elevator and a parking space or garage. Although it would be dripping with old-world charm, the kitchen would be completely modernized, with quartz or granite countertops and stainless steel, commercial-grade appliances. The master bath would include a large soaker tub and a spacious shower (at my request) surrounded by sleek tile and glass. There would be hardwood floors everywhere except the bedrooms, though the bathrooms would probably have travertine tile. It would definitely have central air and heat, and most likely at least a small fireplace. It would be listed at above what she had set as a top limit to her budget, but Edgard had been getting desperate, and Cherie would tell him to negotiate it down as much as possible. It might or might not have a doorman on duty, that feature had been a variable in the past mix of properties. I knew all this because it had become the checklist we had been through countless times as we viewed numerous prospects. I knew it because of Cherie's relentless pursuit of her dream, and her unbridled excitement over this particular find. And I was hopeful that I would love it as well, and that we would find ourselves being very happy there.

A clock chimed somewhere in the interior of the building. Time to see the shrink.

Dr. Guiome concluded our session that day as she often did, by asking about how things were going with Cherie. She usually remained quiet during my reply, nodding and smiling, and I generally considered the inquiry to be more courtesy than therapy.

But that evening she became pensive as I spoke, and I could tell she was putting a great deal of thought into her follow-up to my admittedly trite response.

"Michael, let me speak right now not as your doctor." She gave me an odd, uncharacteristic look. I sensed that this was not easy for her. "I have come to know you well through our time together," she said. "And I have come to understand that you are a man of great passion; *l' emportement*. But I think you are... very cautious. You have much, ah, 'restraint', I think that is the right word."

She paused to think. I was quiet.

"This woman, I think she scares you. No, that is not correct. *Elle te défie*, she 'challenges' you. She makes you want to run away, even as you are drawn to her. Even as you realize that you love her." She looked at me with a warmth she had not displayed before, smiling.

"These are not bad things," she went on, "but they make you *effrayé*... scared? It does not seem orderly for you. But perhaps it is what you need, to be out of order. *L' inconfort*, I would call it. Could it be that you are afraid? Afraid of happiness?"

She paused again, this time studying me, reading my reaction. I put on my best poker face. Her gaze shifted, and I saw her nod almost imperceptibly.

"You should put away your fear, Michael," she said decisively. "You must... take a risk. Allow yourself to put aside *avoir peur*, the fear of what you might regret. Take permission to follow your passion, allow it to bring you pleasure as well as pain. Allow it to lead you to happiness, to love. *Conduisant à l'amour.*" She gave me a satisfied look, assuming I understood the French. I understood her meaning well enough.

Silence filled the room. Her words seemed like more of a speech than a query aimed at soliciting a response, as would be typical of a therapy session. I felt my face flush.

"So, we are done today," she said finally, letting me off the hook. "You will think more about this?"

"Yes, of course," I said, standing "Thank you Doctor."

My head was still swimming with the unsolicited advice as I walked out of the building. It all sounded so... on target? I wasn't sure. Her suggestions, directives really, struck me as potentially irresponsible. Careless. Maybe even dangerous. Okay, that may have been an over-reaction, but it still sounded very "out of character" for me. Heart before head, not a thing I was accustomed to. Then again, she knew that. Which was exactly why she was confronting me with it. Perhaps we would explore it further in our next session. Or perhaps she intended to let me take it from there. Perhaps I would have to ponder that later. I tucked it away for further consideration. At least I tried to.

FIFTY-FIVE

The woman approached the café table and noticed the shopping bag next to the chair. Ignoring it, she sat down, placing her purse behind her feet, under the chair. She looked around self-consciously, uncomfortable in her surroundings. She searched for a waitress, unsure whether there would be one, wondering if she instead needed to go up to the counter inside the doors to place her order. She opted to wait, pulled out her phone and took a picture of the quaint Parisian scene in front of her.

Another woman, holding a white cup with steam swirling above it, approached her table, motioning toward the bag on the ground. "I'm sorry, but I was sitting here," she said.

"Oh, I apologize," said the first woman. She glanced around the café, seeing that all the tables were occupied.

"It's alright," said the second woman. "We can sit here together, if you don't mind."

"Oh, not at all. I'm happy for the company. Here, was this your chair?" She started to rise.

"No, no. Stay put. I can sit over here." She moved the shopping bag over next to the chair on the opposite side of the table. She placed her cup of latte onto the tabletop and sat down.

"Do I order inside?"

"You can, if you don't want to wait. The waitresses here are very slow."

At that moment, despite the warning to the contrary, a waitress stepped up to the table. "*Bonjour, Mademoiselles,*" she said cheerfully. "What can I bring you?"

"I have mine," said the second woman.

"Oh, a coffee for me, I guess," the first woman said, smiling at the waitress.

"*Oui*." The waitress turned and moved to another table, scribbling on her order pad.

"The lighting on that building across the way is so lovely, the way it illuminates the flags," said the first woman, gesturing with her phone toward the scene across the square she had just taken a photo of. "I was just taking a picture."

"Oh, yes," said the second woman, turning to look over her shoulder. "This is one of my favorite spots, at just this time in the evening."

The two women continued to talk, and eventually the waitress delivered the coffee, collecting payment. "*Merci beaucoup*," the waitress said as she turned from the table. The women resumed their conversation, animated and laughing. One would never have guessed they had just met.

Fifteen minutes later, the tranquil scene erupted into chaos as a man in black military-type clothing stepped onto the sidewalk near the outdoor tables, pulled an automatic rifle from beneath his heavy jacket, snapped the stock into place, and began firing. The gunshots were deafening in the crowded square, and people immediately began running, screaming and falling. He shouted "*Allahu Akbar*!" as he continued firing in short bursts, pointing the gun at various different targets in and around the café. People fell to the ground, hit by the bullets. Some writhed and moaned, others lay still. As people began to scatter in all directions, the man pulled a device from beneath his coat, pressing a button on its surface with his left thumb. He looked confused, pressing the button several more times, staring intently at the device in his hand. Exasperated, he dropped the rifle. As it clattered to the ground, he began pressing the button with the thumbs of both hands, backing out into the street as he did so. In a final effort, he banged on the device with his closed fist, stared at it a moment, then shoved it back into his jacket and ran down a narrow alley, away from the scene. The entire incident had transpired in less than a minute, but it clearly altered the world for everyone in the square. Death, fear and disturbing sounds lingered like smoke in the aftermath.

FIFTY-SIX

After finishing my session with Dr. Guiome, I switched my phone ringer on and checked the time. There was a text message on the screen from Cherie, saying she had set up the appointment with Edgard for the next morning, and asking me to meet her for dinner. That was fine, however the logistics were a little tough. She would be waiting for me at one of our favorite cafés, in the 10th Arrondissement, but it was a difficult commute from Dr. Guiome's office. I could take the Metro, but would end up having to go around in a big loop to get to my destination. I could also walk, but it wasn't just a short stroll. The weather was unusually mild for an evening in November, so I opted to walk. I sent Cherie a text, telling her I was on my way, but that it would take me a little while. She texted back a smiley face in response.

I set out and realized quickly that much of the trip would be uphill. No problem, my inner electronics had been working well. After a couple of brisk blocks, I was slightly winded, but didn't feel the need to stop and rest.

At about the mid-point in my journey, I approached a small pub which had televisions mounted above the outdoor seating areas and saw groups of people gathered around two of the TV screens. I could see from the display that it was a special news report. I stopped to take a look.

"What's going on?" I asked the man standing next to me, hoping he spoke English.

"Terrorists," he said curtly. "They are at it again."

I watched the screen as it showed a scene outside the Stade

de France, where a soccer match was being played that night. As I watched the jumbled video on the screen, I recalled a strange booming sound just minutes earlier that had seemed out of place on a peaceful Paris evening. "Not possible," I thought to myself. The scene on the television devolved into chaos, and the video feed was lost, leaving the screen black for a few seconds before switching to a befuddled news anchor, unaware that he was on air. He gave the camera a startled look and then muttered a short statement, shaking his head and shuffling papers on the desk in front of him.

"Bombs!" A woman toward the front of the group said in horror. "They are setting off bombs!" The crowd, which had grown considerably, collectively gasped and murmured in low tones as the video feed came back, returning to the location outside the stadium, where it was clear that there were injured people laying on the ground, with others trying to assist them, or running in the opposite direction. The cameraman was being jostled by the crowd, and the picture was focused on the ground for several seconds before framing an on-air reporter fighting to stand his ground in the moving crowd. He pressed his finger to his ear, listening to an audio feed. He regained some of his composure as he faced the camera and held his microphone in front of him. From his rattled demeanor I guessed that he had shown up prepared to cover a sporting event, not a terrorist attack.

His report was in French and most of it went past me without understanding until I heard the words "*Café Bonne Bière*" come out of his mouth.

"What did he say?" I asked the man next to me. "What about Café Bonne Bière?"

"I'm not certain," the man replied. "I think he said something about some shooting there."

Time stopped. My mouth went dry. I could hear my pulse pounding in my ears, drowning out the considerable noise around me. Café Bonne Bière was my destination. It was where Cherie was waiting for me. For just a second, my feet were frozen to the concrete, my eyes glued to the television screen. The next, my feet were moving, the adrenaline coursing through my body and propelling me into the street and around the corner at a dead run. I weaved in and out of people, occasionally bumping my way past someone and throwing a breathless *"pardon"* in my wake. My legs churned, my arms pumped, my feet struggled for purchase on the uneven surfaces of the streets and sidewalks. I dodged cars as I crossed streets without looking, paying no heed to the traffic signals. I became aware of a strange feeling in my chest as I ran, a burning sensation that went from the point where my device had been implanted, downward toward the center of my chest.

"Not now," I heard myself mumbling. "Don't choose right now to do your thing." I recalled some descriptions I had read online from people whose internal defibrillators had gone off. Most described it as feeling like they'd been kicked in the chest by a mule, or something equally dramatic. I did not need that right now. I tried to put it out of mind. It was substituted by an acute awareness of how long the trek seemed to be taking me.

It had been quite some time since I had run that far, that fast. I could feel it taxing my body in every way, but I pushed on, still fueled by the adrenaline. Or fear. Or panic. I didn't care which, I just kept moving. I was aware of another muffled booming sound, this one closer, coming from behind me. Shit. Shit, shit, shit.

I flew around the corner of a building and ran smack into someone else travelling in the opposite direction at almost equal speed. The impact was overpowering, sprawling both of us out into the street. A car honked as brakes squealed and headlights swept over us. I rolled as I fell, consciously avoiding my previously-injured shoulder. I wound up on my side, half-sitting and staring into the face of the man I had run into. He sat in the street, legs splayed, glaring back at me. Dark eyes and hair. Built like a linebacker. Bulky black coat. Sour expression. As I began to rise, and was preparing to apologize, the man reached into his coat and pulled out what looked like a doorbell button wrapped in black electrical tape. There were wires running from the thing back into his coat. He pushed his thumb down on the button repeatedly, looking up at me as he did so.

"Fuckin' bloody hell!" He muttered. I detected an accent, but had no clue as to what kind. People from the sidewalk had been moving toward us to help, but stopped short at that point. A man shouted something in French and held those on either side of him back with his outstretched arms.

I glanced into the eyes of the man on the street in front of me. They swirled with a dark hatred. He pushed again and again on the device, his malice seemingly growing with each maniacal motion. It was clear that he wanted desperately to do harm to anyone and everyone around him as his fingers worked frantically on the object in his hands.

I noticed in all the confusion that something didn't look quite right as I watched his thumbs plunge up and down on the button, and then it hit me: he was missing the index finger of his right hand, making his grip on the device awkward and clumsy.

None of this distracted me from the fact that I was on a mission. I leapt to my feet, forced my way past the bystanders and ran onward, toward the cafe. The frenzied man shouted something from behind me. I did not look back.

By the time I turned onto Rue de la Fontaine-au-Roi, I was beyond winded. My legs burned, my chest heaved, my back spasmed with sharp pains, my feet throbbed, and I had a splitting headache. And still, the burning in my chest. I could almost trace the fiery sensation along the veins en route to my heart, the feeling was so distinct. I reached up and pressed my right hand against my coat, on top of the left breast pocket, almost expecting to feel heat radiating outward through my clothing.

I saw the square where the café was located in the distance, a block ahead. I squinted with concentration and tried to recall what Cherie had been wearing earlier in the day. A white silk blouse and lightweight navy jacket. Tan pants. Keep running.

As I neared the scene, my dread was only compounded. It was evident that something awful had happened. People were running around in confusion and things did not look right. My brain struggled to process my initial assessment. Overturned furniture. Debris everywhere. Broken glass. Sirens approaching. And people laying on the ground, some moving, some not. Rancid smells that were not normal. My eyes desperately scanned the area for Cherie's clothing, hair, face. My panic rose as I could not find any of them. Then my ears took over.

"Oh my god, Michael!" It was Cherie's voice, strained and panicked, but undoubtedly hers. I looked toward the sound, and saw her crouched against the side of a building behind a low wall that bordered the square. I was flooded with relief, overcome with a sense of joy that was in direct contradiction to the revulsion generated by the ghastly scene in front of me. I ran to where Cherie was huddled and scooped her into my arms. She bent her head against my chest, hyperventilating. I stroked her hair gently, willing her breathing to return to normal. I turned my head so that I could stare at the horrifying vision behind us.

"Shhh," I said quietly into her ear. "Shhh. It will be alright."

FIFTY-SEVEN

"That poor woman," Cherie said quietly. She had calmed down, but was still distraught. We were sitting on the wall near the café. The police had directed that anyone present at the time of the shooting should remain until they could be interviewed. It was going very slowly. I looked down at the backs of her hands, where gauze squares had been applied by a paramedic who had treated her for cuts from flying glass and debris. There were also small cuts on the side of her face that had been cleaned, but not bandaged. Her slacks were torn at the knee, and there was grime and dried blood staining the fabric around the jagged hole, splatters trailing down her pantleg.

"I need to know what happened to her," she said, grabbing my hand.

"Tell me about it again," I said. "Maybe we can ask someone while we're waiting, see if they can give us any information."

"She was so kind," Cherie went on, rubbing her eyes. "The café was full, so we shared a table. I had gone to pick up my order, and she was sitting there when I got back." I could see her eyes welling up with tears. "She was sitting in my chair, Michael. If she had not been there, I would have been sitting right where she was. It would have been me..." The statement trailed off into sobs.

"And you didn't see her again after... after things happened?"

"Just lying on the ground as I ran away." Her voice was steeped in anger, frustration and self-judgment.

"It's not your fault, Cherie. You had to protect yourself. You had good instincts." She snorted in response, wiped at her nose with a tissue.

"I need to know what happened," she repeated.

"Okay, you sit tight. I'll see if I can find someone that might be able to help us. Are you sure you're not cold?" The previously mild evening was turning chilly. The square was illuminated unnaturally by huge klieg lights, but they provided no warmth.

"No, I'm fine," she replied, pulling a gendarme's cloak that a caring officer had provided up around her shoulders. I squeezed her hand and walked off toward what seemed to be the staging area.

The snippets of conversation we overheard around the scene were almost exclusively about the other, seemingly related, events which had transpired within a 40-minute window during the evening. The bombings at the Stade de France that I had seen on television had started things off. Later, a shooting spree at another bar and restaurant, also in the 10th Arrondissement. Shortly thereafter, a devastating hail of automatic weapon fire at La Belle Equipe on Rue de Charonne, then a suicide bomber on Boulevard Voltaire. And finally, a scene of unfathomable carnage at a sold-out concert in Bataclan Hall. No one seemed to know how many had died in total, but the rumors were that it was in the dozens, or even hundreds. It was almost too much to take in all at once. I tried to focus on the terror right in front of me, our personal good fortune, and my hope that it was all over.

I located a gendarme that looked like he was in a position of authority, a sergeant or the equivalent, perhaps. He had a clipboard in his hand and seemed to be directing the activity around him. Dressed in full riot gear, he was very focused and intense, to the point that I was hesitant to approach him. When I sensed a pause in the action and found a moment to step in front of him, he was surprisingly patient and willing to help, given the chaotic scene. I gave him the description and information about the woman that Cherie had given me, and pointed out the location of the table, according to Cherie's recollection. He perused his clipboard, quickly jotted down a couple of notes and said he would get back with me. I showed him where we were waiting, and told him that I would let him know if we moved, or were allowed to leave. He nodded and gave me a look that I interpreted as: "Believe me, you're not going anywhere soon."

I inexplicably found myself looking around for Chief Malboeuf. It didn't make sense, I knew, given the scope of that evening's catastrophes, for him to be at that particular scene, but I looked for his familiar form nonetheless. I wondered what he would make of the coincidence that Cherie and I had been peripherally involved in yet another terrorist incident. I also thought, perhaps more realistically, that Gregor might show up, but again, there was far too much activity in the city that night for him to have become aware of our involvement. He had been maintaining a very low profile of late, especially after the divorce had been finalized, but I was relatively sure that we would eventually be hearing from him.

FIFTY-EIGHT

Death wandered amidst the chaos outside of the Stade de France. He wore a crinkled white hazmat suit, complete with hood, plastic visor with a breathing mask, and white booties over his shoes. Stepping carefully, he moved among the people remaining after the initial destruction. Tableaus of terror, shock and pain played out across the car park and grounds of the Stade. He turned slowly toward the sound of a woman pleading for help, her hands on the chest of a man on the ground who was pale and unmoving. He turned away, stepping over a pile of debris that had spilled from an overturned garbage can. He adjusted the mask and breathing apparatus so that he could see better, then ducked under a damaged steel railing and entered the stadium complex.

He moved carefully up a concrete ramp as gendarmes and emergency personnel milled around him, paying him no mind. He made his way through a short tunnel and emerged onto a concrete platform overlooking the interior of the structure. There were hundreds of people gathered on the green pitch, huddled together in fear, held in place by security officers and police, anxiously watching and listening for additional explosions outside the walls. They seemed to be unaware, or at least unwilling to acknowledge, that the danger could come from within as well.

He turned away, disinterested in the crowd milling on the turf. He retraced his steps back out to the exterior of the stadium, once again ignoring the chaos, and maneuvered away from the crowds, noise and activity, pausing occasionally to glance at prone or seated figures, some of them writhing in pain. He worked his way to the outer perimeter which had been established by police and emergency vehicles around the edge of the parking area, red and blue lights flashing, turning the darkness into a nightmarish kaleidoscope. He slipped between two ambulances, stripping off the hazmat suit and leaving it on the front bumper of one of them. The stark contrast between the white protective material and his dark blazer was striking. He adjusted his jacket, shrugging it up onto his narrow shoulders, automatically reaching to his collar to straighten his tie. He brushed away some white fibers left behind by the suit from his sleeve, and wound his way through the maze of media vehicles parked haphazardly beyond the emergency perimeter. A block away, he settled into his car, the white booties still covering his shoes. He pulled them from his leather loafers and tossed them out of the open top as he pulled away from the curb.

FIFTY-NINE

I am seated on a stone wall outside of Café Bonne Bière, where Rue de la Fontaine-au-Roi intersects with Rue du Faubourg du Temple, in the 10th Arrondissement. I have my arm around Cherie, and she has a traditional gendarme's blue wool cape draped across her back. She is shaking and sobbing quietly, her face pressed tightly against her cupped hands, her body convulsing under my firm grip. She has just experienced something more horrific than I can even imagine.

I look around at the scene in front of us as I rub her shoulder, pulling her close to me. There are police everywhere, medical personnel frantically attending to injured people, onlookers behind the blue tape strung haphazardly around the scene, kept at bay by patient but firm gendarmes now lining the perimeter of the area. Tables and chairs from the café are scattered around the sidewalk, broken glass glimmers sharply in the artificial light, and there are several bodies covered by white cloth. Blood stains spread in drying patterns on the concrete around them, seeping up into the edges of the fabric. The scene is one of death and devastation that defies the limits of our insulated experience. Cherie leans closer and buries her face into my chest.

In that moment, something breaks loose inside me, like sand before a wave. I realize that there is no such thing as perfection in this world, that this time, this place, this woman, are all that I need to be happy, to be complete. I swear that I will not let this feeling pass, that I will remain fully engaged, as Bob used to say, and relish in the joy that has fallen into my lap. I have wasted too much time in the middle lane, afraid of swerving left or right for fear of the traffic speeding past me on both sides. To hell with it, I decide, pick a lane and push the pedal down, see where it takes you, caution be damned.

I tighten my grip on Cherie's shoulder, to the point where I'm afraid I might hurt her. She continues to shake, and I hold on for dear life.

SIXTY

"Are you sure you are not mistaken?" the gendarme sergeant asked patiently, flipping through the pages on his clipboard. "Perhaps she was not hit."

"No, no, I saw her get shot," Cherie said, frustrated, her jaw set in a stubborn clench that I had become familiar with. "She was sitting right across the table from me, less than a meter away. Then she was on the ground, bleeding badly. There was a lot of blood." She paused, glancing down at the leg of her pants. I suspected that some of that blood had ended up there. "I tried to reach her, to help her, but I had to move away because of the gunfire. The bullets were spraying glass and wood... everywhere." She held up one of her bandaged hands, gently touching the cuts on her face. "I took cover behind the wall, and the last I saw she was lying there where our table had been." She pointed vaguely in the direction of the café. "There was a lot of blood."

"I am sorry, Madame," the gendarme said sincerely. "But I show no record of an American woman such as you have described being injured or killed. We have been very carefully documenting those involved, especially the, ah...," he glanced at me furtively, "...foreigners. I have a list of all those who have been transported by ambulance or attended to on scene by the medics, including yourself. Are you sure she was an American?"

"Yes, yes," Cherie replied, exasperated. "She was American. She told me so, that she had just arrived here from the U.S."

"Is there anything else you recall? Her name, perhaps?"

Cherie looked toward the ground, shaking her head back and forth slightly.

"Madame," said the gendarme, "I will update my list, and then..."

"Wait!" Cherie said, raising her head suddenly, the recollection hitting her. "She told me her name. She said it was Patricia." She pointed her index finger at the gendarme. "She told me her name was Patricia." I saw her eyes widen, and she turned her head slowly to look at me.

My heart skipped a beat, recovered, then skipped another.

SIXTY-ONE

*W*e are lounging comfortably on the sofa in the sitting room of Cherie's old house, a fire crackling in the hearth, rain pelting the window panes. Cherie is engrossed in a book and I am wrestling with the New York Times crossword puzzle. The house has been taken off the market, at least temporarily, and our new home search has similarly been halted. Cherie's reaction to the shooting at Café Bonne Bière has been intense and lingering, and the events of that evening have had a similar effect on the population of Paris. There is a communal sense of dread that can't be shaken, and Cherie's mood has followed that inclination.

I have felt it too. The black dog is gone, has been for some time, this is about something else. I share the shocked reaction which has overtaken France, Europe, and even the world in the aftermath of the tragedies of the past year. It feels as if time has frozen, and our lives have followed a parallel pattern.

The lack of momentum has not affected everything. We have just returned from a post-Holiday trip to the States, where my kids embraced Cherie with unequivocal warmth and acceptance, due in part to some effective advance work carried out by Lauren. I have been able to sort out nearly all of the issues related to my practice, visa status and insurance coverage with amazing rapidity. Nothing gets results like being able to physically park yourself in front of someone and assuring them that you are not going anywhere until something is resolved. So, our return to Paris was infused with a sense of completion, satisfaction and permanence. But it was a homecoming to a place filled with unease, and Cherie and I are not immune to it.

As an American, my experience with the specter of international terrorism has been defined by 9/11, the World Trade Center attack in New York. It is our national touchstone of loss, of disbelief, and of horror. It was a devastating, callously inflicted injury that threatened to bring our country to its knees. It impacted each and every one of us in profound ways, first with raw fear, then with determination and resolve. Those eventual reactions, however, had not been immediate. We first needed to grapple with our collective grief, to shake ourselves awake from the paralyzing nightmare that descended upon us during that sunny morning in September. It is a feeling that I now recall and recognize.

I put down my paper and pat Cherie's bare foot, which is pressed against my thigh beneath the wool blanket that we share. I stare out the window, focused absently on the fat drops of rain as they trail down the glass. I am anxious for this chilly spell of Paris winter to pass, anticipating the glorious springtime that compares with nothing else in the world. I long for the rebirth of the city, the country, its inhabitants, their spirit. For this devastated society working so hard to repair itself, to heal.

I see with new clarity that the entirety of Europe is an ailing patient, stricken with a debilitating illness, fighting to recover, laboring with all its energy against a force that it cannot comprehend, contain or eliminate. It is a force which I have encountered before, and that I know can be defeated.

I squeeze Cherie's foot and she looks up at me quizzically, her hazel eyes suddenly alight with a spark that has been absent, one that I have missed. It makes my heart soar, and gives me hope for the struggling patient. I can envision the recovery.

If London is the brain, and Germany the powerful muscle,

then Paris is the beating heart of Europe. It has pulsed along for centuries, supplying nourishment for the soul needed by the citizens to make them whole, give them the essence of life, a passion which drives them to bigger and better things, ideas, realities. This past year that steady rhythm was interrupted twice, was shocked into silence for a beat or two, just long enough to cause us to catch our collective breath, to raise an unsteady hand to our chest in fear. But the syncopation of those moments became a terrifying yet productive pause where we stopped to compose ourselves, steeling our resolve to confront whatever events the future might reveal. The heartbeat was re-established, the pulse resumed, and life moved on, giving us the ability to push forward, more determined than ever to prevail in the timeless struggle against malevolence and destruction.

CPSIA information can be obtained
at www.ICGtesting.com
Printed in the USA
FSHW021642260820
73248FS